DYING TO GET HER MAN

DYING TO GET HER MAN

Judy Fitzwater

Thorndike Press • Chivers Press
Waterville, Maine USA   Bath, England

This Large Print edition is published by Thorndike Press, USA and by Chivers Press, England.

Published in 2002 in the U.S. by arrangement with The Ballantine Publishing Group, a division of Random House, Inc.

Published in 2002 in the U.K. by arrangement with The Ballantine Publishing Group, a division of Random House, Inc.

U.S. Softcover 0-7862-4587-5 (Paperback Series)
U.K. Hardcover 0-7540-7466-8 (Chivers Large Print)
U.K. Softcover 0-7540-7467-6 (Camden Large Print)

The text of this Large Print edition is unabridged. Other aspects of the book may vary from the original edition.

Set in 16 pt. Plantin.

Printed in the United States on permanent paper.

British Library Cataloguing-in-Publication Data available

Library of Congress Cataloging-in-Publication Data

Fitzwater, Judy.
Dying to get her man / Judy Fitzwater.
p. cm.
ISBN 0-7862-4587-5 (lg. print : sc : alk. paper)
1. Marsh, Jennifer (Fictitious character) — Fiction.
2. Women novelists — Fiction. 3. Large type books.
I. Title.
PS3556.I899 D93 2002
813′.54—dc21 2002075966

For Larry
Today, tomorrow,
and all the days after that

Thanks, once again, to the talented people whose help and support make my books possible: Larry, Miellyn, and Anastasia; Patricia Peters and Joe Blades; Robyn Amos, Ann Kline, Vicki Singer, Karen Smith, and Pat Gagne.

I couldn't do it without you.

Chapter 1

Love can kill. Suzanne Gray proved it two days ago when she dressed herself all in white, drew back her dark hair with a blue ribbon, gathered a bouquet of white roses, and spread a linen cloth across Richard Hovey's grave. Then she turned on a tape of "All You Need Is Love," swallowed a bottle of sleeping pills, and lay down to join him on the coldest day in Macon, Georgia's recent history, and froze to death, leaving only the shadow of a smile on her lips.

Now all of Macon was talking about her death, including a deejay on a local radio station not thirty minutes ago, just as Jennifer Marsh and Sam Culpepper had pulled into the parking lot of the Casablanca Club.

With thoughts of Suzanne in mind, Jennifer was not at all certain how she felt about "until death do us part" or how she intended to handle what she feared Sam was about to say as he gently brushed back her long, taffy brown hair. He kissed her shoulder on either side of her spaghetti strap and drew her close on the restaurant's dance floor, the ominous strains of "How Do I Live Without You" in the background.

He'd seemed far too serious when he called to make a date for Saturday night and spoke those most dreaded of words, "We need to talk." If this was it, the big will-you-marry-me, she wasn't about to tell him no, but she sure wasn't ready to say yes. Not yet. Not until she had achieved at least some promise of success as a writer. All she needed was one contract for any of her mystery novels, or some other small acknowledgment of her talents.

After all, Sam was a well known investigative reporter for the *Macon Telegraph.* He'd even written several acclaimed feature articles, including one about Richard Hovey. The article had garnered so much attention that Hovey had asked him to co-author his memoirs. Of course that was before Hovey died. And before Suzanne had killed herself on his grave. What Sam planned to do now, only he knew — about the Hovey book *and* about his and Jennifer's relationship.

There was a slim possibility, she supposed, that what Sam wanted to say had nothing to do with them as a couple.

He nuzzled her neck, sending little sparks down her spine.

Yeah, right. She gazed about the room. Candlelight, superb wine, a four-course dinner at one of Macon's trendiest restaurants, carrying a price tag equivalent to an entire night's catering for Dee Dee, bare tree branches wrapped in twinkling white lights reflected in floor-to-ceiling windows, cloth napkins, and tuxedoed waiters. The man was serious.

"Jennifer," he whispered, his breath hot in her ear, as they swayed to the music. Sam didn't actually dance, but he swayed with the best of them. "We've known each other for some time now. You know how —"

Suddenly Suzanne's death seemed of paramount importance and a far safer subject than whatever Sam was about to say.

"Did you see the body?" Jennifer asked.

"Oh, yeah. And lookin' really good, too." He cocked his head against hers. "That doesn't sound like a question you'd ask."

Jennifer felt a blush sweep across her neck and down her chest. "I *meant* Suzanne Gray's body."

He drew back and stared at her, his dark hair falling across his right eyebrow just the way she liked it. Then he pulled her close to him again, the fresh scent of his aftershave spicing her thoughts. She could have stayed like that forever, so comfortable in his arms. Too comfortable.

"You don't want to know about that," Sam whispered. "We have something we need to —"

Not so comfortable after all.

Jennifer jerked back. "Oh, yes, I do. Tell me about the flowers."

He sighed. "I suppose it'd be too much to hope you're talking about the roses I brought you tonight."

"Suzanne's flowers."

"Jennifer . . ."

"I want to know. Please just humor me." She teased his lip with her finger. Not a good idea. She managed to snatch it away before he kissed it.

Sam frowned. "They were clutched in her hands. Frozen. Like she was. All that was in the article I wrote for the newspaper. I know you read it. So why are you asking?"

Thank goodness. He was off topic now, and the spell he'd tried so hard to cast had been broken.

"It just seems so sad. A woman dying alone in the cemetery all because of that

Richard Hovey. Not the nicest man this city has ever laid claim to."

Sam didn't need to know that even she'd felt a flutter whenever Hovey's photo splashed across the TV screen, which was pretty often what with his death seven days ago and then, just yesterday, the release of one of his most notorious clients, Simon DeSoto. There was no denying Hovey had charisma, charm, even good looks. Too bad he had no morals.

"He was a good lawyer," Sam reminded her.

"If by 'good,' you mean he almost always won, you're right. And I'll admit that if I were ever in trouble — and guilty — he'd be the one I'd want defending me."

"That'd be quite a trick now that he's dead."

Sam swung her around into a dip.

She frowned at him and pulled herself back up. "Don't change the subject. I was talking about Suzanne. The poor woman was found by some groundskeeper. How old was she again?"

"Thirty-nine."

Nine years older than Jennifer.

"She had a lot of life yet to live. Why would she give up like that, not even try —"

"She's not the only one not trying,"

Sam pointed out.

Oh, she was trying all right, and apparently succeeding. At least he was answering her questions. "Did she leave a suicide note?"

"She had on some kind of lacy gloves. It was tucked inside the right one, next to her palm."

Suddenly Jennifer really was more interested in Suzanne than in diverting Sam. "You didn't mention that in the article, and I haven't heard one word about it on any of the news reports. What did it say?"

"It said that she was so nuts about Richard that she couldn't live without him."

"The nuts part I'll go along with. Was it common knowledge that they were involved?"

"No," Sam assured her. "Before Hovey's death, I'd never heard of her. He didn't mention her during the interviews he gave me for the book. Pretty much no one knew they were engaged, at least not until they were both dead."

"Well, they know it now. They're calling her the Bride Who Died," Jennifer told him.

"Yeah, I think we've got the *Atlanta Eye* to thank for that catchy phrase."

"So you didn't know about the engagement when you were covering the story of her death."

"Oh, I knew. Shirley over at the style section made sure I knew. But her section had already gone to print carrying the announcement — in the same edition of the *Telegraph* that my article about Suzanne's death appeared in."

"Then why didn't you include it?"

"Hovey's family asked that we downplay the relationship, which they were totally unaware of — and which they deny. Out of respect for them and both Hovey and Gray, I haven't reported it in any subsequent articles. Too easy to let controversy overtake the tragedy. I didn't want that to happen. But it does appear he was expecting Suzanne the night he died."

"And just how do you know that?" Jennifer demanded, louder than she intended to. "Sam, you may hold out on the reading public, but not on me. Now spill."

Sam pulled her closer, his hand pressing against the small of her back, and spoke directly into her ear. "I'm telling you this for only one reason: so you'll understand what happened and let it go. Agreed?"

She made a noncommittal nod of her head.

"Agreed?" he repeated.

"Okay, okay. Just tell me."

"You know that Richard Hovey died from a fall at his home."

"Of course. He slipped on the stairs. The fall broke his neck."

"Right. He slipped on rose petals."

She pulled back. "Rose petals?" she said out loud. He shushed her and pulled her back to him.

She whispered, "What were rose petals doing on the stairs?"

"When the police arrived at Hovey's townhouse, they found a trail of red petals leading from the top of the stairs into the bedroom, where the path split. Some petals led to the king-size bed, others to the bathroom and a tub of water where oils and more petals were floating. There were candles, too, burned well into their wax at the landing, on top of the bedroom dresser, and on the counter in the bathroom. Oh, and a bottle of Silver Oak cabernet sauvignon and two wineglasses next to the bed."

"How romantic."

"Yeah," Sam agreed, "until you add an aromatic corpse to the mix."

That did take some of the magic away.

"The police concluded that Hovey was

expecting a woman Saturday night, had created the scene, and then slipped on a small pile of petals on the slick hardwood floor at the top of the stairs. His feet flew out from under him, and down the stairs he went."

"How horrible," Jennifer said. "No wonder Suzanne was devastated. Here she was expecting to . . . to . . . well, you know, but instead . . . Did she call the police?"

"No. The doors were locked. If she came to his house, she must not have come in. The police didn't know about Suzanne. None of his friends or family gave them her name, and she didn't come forward so she was never questioned. And, as I said, none of us in the media knew about her until she died herself. He was discovered Monday morning when his cleaning service arrived and let themselves in."

"How did you manage to keep the story quiet? Surely the cleaning crew saw the petals."

"They didn't go upstairs, and Hovey's fall had taken most of the ones on the stairs down with him. Besides, Hovey had been lying there long enough that I doubt they noticed anything but his body. The smell had to be unbelievable. If they did see petals, they were shriveled, and I'm sure they didn't catch the significance."

She could have done without the image of Hovey's decaying body. "You didn't print any of this in the newspaper."

"It seemed only right to leave the man some privacy."

"And so — her lover dead — Suzanne killed herself, and no one even knew they'd ever been in love."

"Well-known people sometimes have private affairs. He died and she obviously had a difficult time dealing with it. Most likely she had unresolved issues, things left unsaid. She may have even blamed herself for his death, for not getting to his house earlier, or for him putting together the evening in the first place. You know, the usual stuff. Survivor's guilt."

"Just how usual do you think this sort of thing is?" Jennifer demanded, offended as she was certain Suzanne would have been.

"It happens," he assured her. "Two people leave important things unsaid . . ."

There he was, trying to make this personal again. "When did she write the suicide note? It would have been awfully cold and dark out there at his grave."

"Presumably at home. It was typewritten or printed —"

Jennifer broke Sam's grip and took a

step back. "It was printed, as in not written by hand? What about the signature?"

"It wasn't signed. It's pretty obvious —"

"That she may not have written it," Jennifer insisted loudly just as the music stopped. "Sam, what if Suzanne Gray was murdered?"

Chapter 2

Sam pasted on a fake grin and spoke through clenched teeth, never moving a lip, nodding at the other dancers who'd all stopped to stare. "Suzanne Gray committed suicide. She wasn't murdered."

He took her back into his arms as the strains of "With or Without You" started up. He actually tried a kind of waltzing turn step that had nothing whatsoever to do with the beat of the music. She was having none of it.

Jennifer lowered her voice, both feet firmly planted on the ground. "Maybe. Maybe not. But who would forget to sign a suicide note? All those preparations and she doesn't even write her name? How'd you even know who she was?"

Sam closed his eyes, obviously aware of what was about to come. "Her name was typed."

"Like some business letter signature?" Jennifer just shook her head. "You're not going to convince me that you don't think something fishy is going on, something other than suicide, Sam. You know better. Richard Hovey was into all sorts of specious activity. Lord knows what part of the primordial slime his clients crawled out of. I'll give you his fall on the stairs — I can't really see gangsters strewing rose petals and lighting candles — but what if Suzanne got mixed up in some of his goings-on? What if she found out something she wasn't supposed to know? What if, with Richard dead, she felt no obligation to keep what she knew to herself? What if she decided to blackmail —"

"Put a rein on that overactive writer's imagination of yours," he told her. "In your books, of course Suzanne would have been murdered, but this is real life. Her man died. She killed herself. It's no more complicated than that."

He paused, obviously waiting for her to reply, but all she did was stare at him. "Look, the police believe her death to be a suicide. Let's leave it at that. Did you get any writing done today."

Now he was trying to distract her, but she wasn't about to let him beat her at her own game. "Sam Culpepper, you know better. If Suzanne loved Richard Hovey enough to kill herself, she would have tucked that suicide note next to her heart, not in her glove. And even if she did put it in her right glove, she'd most likely have been left-handed. Was she?"

"Not according to her sister." He was already a step ahead of her. "But Suzanne did have terrible handwriting, which might explain —"

"Ah hah! Sam, if we let this woman's murder go unsolved, we'll . . . we'll be abetting her murderer."

"Whoa!" Sam took her hand and led her to their table. People were staring again. "I bear no responsibility for anyone's actions except my own. And neither do you."

"I'm sorry. I didn't mean to imply it's your fault that she's dead," she assured him as she sat and Sam pushed in her chair. As soon as he took his seat, she leaned forward and whispered loudly, "But it may be our fault — assuming she was killed by some criminal — that her murderer isn't caught if we don't even consider the possibility and investigate." Drat. That wasn't much better. "I mean we just can't ignore —"

"I'm not ignoring anything," Sam assured her, placing his napkin on his lap and refilling her wineglass.

Sam motioned to the waiter, who was

immediately at their table. “Do you think you could speed up our entrées?”

“I’ll check on them right away.” Then he disappeared, as a good waiter should.

She studied his face. No smile, just that piercing stare of his, and she immediately understood. He had already considered the possibility that Suzanne Gray could have been murdered. He suspected it the moment he’d seen the note, but he hadn’t written his suspicions in the newspaper, and he hadn’t told her.

“I’m looking into it,” Sam confessed, “but I can’t imagine anyone going to such lengths to stage a death like that one if it wasn’t suicide.”

“Of course not. Don’t you see? That’s why it’s even more probable Suzanne’s death was murder.”

“Only in mystery novels. Jennifer . . . trust me on this one.”

He was definitely holding out on her. “You intend to go forward with the book about Hovey, don’t you?”

“Hovey’s ex-wife Ruth has agreed to cooperate. She’s releasing some of his papers to me as soon as she’s had a chance to go through them.”

Her mind was racing. “Without Hovey to censor what you write and with all the media attention surrounding his and Suzanne's deaths, this could be big, couldn't it, Sam? I mean with Hovey's notoriety, the interviews you had with him, and his ex-wife's cooperation, if you do turn up something that proves Suzanne's death wasn't suicide . . . or even if it was, it has a kind of Romeo-and-Juliet spin."

"Let's not get ahead of ourselves. Ruth Hovey may try to influence the book as the price for her help, and my take is that she'll want as little included about Suzanne Gray as possible."

"What's up with her?"

"She fought the divorce."

"Even more interesting. This could actually be a career maker, Sam, like *All the President's Men* was for Woodward and Bernstein."

"Hardly like —"

"You could probably do it even without Ruth's cooperation if she gets too tyrannical. This would be a much bigger true crime book than *The Channel Fourteen Murders* that we wrote together and that the publisher wouldn't let me put my name on. We could do this one together, too, only this time —"

"We?"

"You'll need me on this one," she told

him, sitting back and taking a sip of the full-bodied red wine. It had already begun to give her a headache, but it was worth it. "You need someone to represent Suzanne's feelings, someone to tell you how a woman thinks."

"Jennifer, you don't think like anybody — man or woman — that I've ever met."

She grinned at him. "I'll take that as a compliment, however it was intended. We'll need an 'in' to Suzanne's part of the story. We should interview her friends, her coworkers. You mentioned a sister."

"Marjorie Turner. She hates journalists and the way some of the newspapers have sensationalized her sister's death, but for some reason she likes me." He grinned.

"That's because you're fair and honest and have really cute knees."

"I don't think Mrs. Turner has had an opportunity to view my knees."

"More's the pity. She has no idea what she's missing. What's this sister like?"

"Middle-aged, married. Not my type."

"Good. With lots of gray hair, I hope. It's great that she trusts you. So you admit Suzanne's death is a possible murder?"

"Absolutely not. The note is an irregularity, but there were no signs of struggle."

"Fill me with a bottle of sleeping pills

and I won't struggle either."

"Don't tempt me. It's not easy to get that kind of dose into someone, certainly not without their knowledge. An empty pill bottle was found at the scene, so the assumption is she took the pills willingly."

"Did they check for fingerprints?"

"That I don't know, but I would think so even though Suzanne was wearing gloves. An autopsy is being performed despite a request that one not be."

"Let me guess; that was in the typed note, too. Who would think to include something like that in a suicide note except a murderer? No bruises, no marks on the body?"

"None."

"Where did her dress come from? Was it new?"

"That I don't know."

"And you didn't ask. That's a question only a woman would think of. We need to check the label. Was it an actual wedding dress?"

"No, of course not. Why would it be?"

"White dress, a bouquet of white roses, blue ribbon, and now you've added lace gloves and a note confessing her undying love. Satin shoes?"

"Yep."

"It equals a wedding, Sam, if not in this life then in the next. Why do you think they're calling her the Bride Who Died? As I said, we need to find out about the dress. If it was an old dress, that's one thing. But if she bought it new, we need to ask the clerk who sold it to her if she said anything. If we're lucky, Suzanne will have told her all about her plans — that is, if she bought it for her wedding to Richard. And if it was after his death, heaven knows what she said."

"I told you it wasn't a wedding dress. It was plain, simple, sleeveless, linen, I think."

"And the flowers," Jennifer rushed on. "They had to be fresh, so they were definitely post-Richard. As long as she didn't pick them up at Kroger's, a florist may have a record. Buying roses out of season is expensive and takes some planning as you know. Thanks again, by the way. Mine were beautiful.

"Oh, Sam, I can help if you'll only let me," she said. "When we talk to Ruth Hovey, we'll have to ask if she knew about their affair."

"Hard to say what she knows. We'll talk to her, but we'll have to be careful. We don't want to offend her. And I don't want any mention of murder, understood? Suzanne's autopsy report is due back Monday. I'd stake a good-size wager that it won't show anything new. I saw the body. She took pills and she froze to death."

Sam was right, of course. If Suzanne was murdered, this was no hit. Hit men didn't use poison. That was a woman's weapon. She'd mention that to him later, when he was more amenable to the possibility.

"Now, I don't suppose you could possibly relax and simply enjoy what's left of the evening?" he asked.

The waiter set Jennifer's pasta primavera in front of her and then served Sam his prime rib.

"I saw another report on the news about beef."

Sam raised an eyebrow at her.

"Sorry." She attacked her food. Too bad Sam couldn't develop a taste for pasta. It was scrumptious, almost worth what he was paying for it.

She swallowed. "Sam, about Suzanne —"

He shook his head. She wouldn't get more out of him until the autopsy report. She'd managed to break his earlier mood, and now she was sorry she had. She'd wasted their romantic evening together with talk of death and suicide and true-crime books.

But she'd make it up to him. It'd be good for both of them, to actually be working together on an equal basis, solving a crime. With her imagination and his objectivity, they had all the bases covered. This was exactly what had eluded her, the missing element to their relationship, a way for her to prove herself professionally.

And she'd see to it that they would have another evening together soon.

She reached over and grabbed his hand. They sat like that, eating in silence. It would all work out. They had plenty of time to examine their feelings for each other. It didn't have to be tonight. After all, it wasn't as if Sam were going to run off and marry someone else.

Chapter 3

The call woke her at 8:43 the next morning. Her eyes tightly shut, the comforter pulled snugly around her neck to ward off the unusual — at least for Georgia — winter cold, Jennifer groggily fumbled for the phone on her nightstand and pricked her finger on one of the roses Sam had brought her last night. She swore, mumbled a quick apology to God, and reared out of bed. Her eyes popped open to find a dark red droplet of blood forming on her skin. She brushed it away and grabbed the receiver, uttering an irritated hello.

"Your entire future is in danger. You must come this very minute." Elderly Emma Walker's usually sweet and kind voice came across the line with a take-no-prisoners attitude.

"What's wrong?" Jennifer demanded.

"I refuse to answer any questions. Not over the phone. Trust me. It's a matter of the utmost importance. You must get over here at once. Don't take time to eat. I'll give you breakfast when you arrive."

While a bit paranoid, Emma was not one to panic.

"I'm not even awake. I need to —"

"Nothing you could do is more important than this," Mrs. Walker barked, the strength in her voice defying her tiny frame, her patience nonexistent. "We have no time as it is. It will take you over an hour to drive from Macon to Atlanta. Don't you see? We must devise a plan before it's too late. You must get him back."

And then the phone went dead.

"Get him back?" Jennifer repeated to the dial tone, her eyes only half open, her mind barely functioning. She stuck her aching finger in her mouth, mumbling around it, "Get *who* back?"

She shook her head and forced her brain to snap to it. Then she punched in Mrs. Walker's number, but no one, not even the answering machine, would pick up, no matter how many times she pushed redial. Obviously, the woman had unplugged the phone.

Maybe Tiger, that evil beast of a mutated Chihuahua that Mrs. Walker called her dog, had run away. No. That would be too good to be true. Tiger was destined to outlive them all. And in the luxury of his benefactor's more-than-comfortable home.

She rolled out of bed to Muffy's enthusiastic good-morning licks.

"Okay, okay." Jennifer rubbed the greyhound's head and neck. "You get breakfast and a ten-minute walk, and I get a five-minute shower. That will simply have to be good enough." She yawned, stretched, and groaned.

She picked up the offending rose. Its petals were wilted, but she drew it to her nose anyway and smiled. The scent was still sweet. If she'd put it in the vase with the others last night as she should have, it'd still be fresh. But she'd been exhausted by the time she remembered, and now it was too late.

After Sam had brought her home, she'd felt energized. He was actually going to let her work with him on the Hovey book. How could she possibly sleep?

She had stayed up until three in the morning trying to work a frozen corpse found in a graveyard — one couldn't have too many dead bodies in a mystery novel — into her latest book, *Dancing till Dead*. It was a deliciously twisted tale of murder and romance, and *the* story that was going to wow some New York editor and finally

— please God — get her published.

She'd planned to reward her hard work — and her successful dodging of Sam's questions — with at least another hour of sleep before his expected call. They planned to grab some lunch, perhaps even see a movie. There wouldn't be anything new on the Suzanne Gray case — not on a Sunday — so that could wait. After he dropped her back home, she'd wall herself up and begin the laborious task of going through the entire manuscript of her book for one more reading before starting on the conclusion.

She sighed. She really would like that time with Sam, time without talk of murder, suicide, or writing of any kind, time to remind him and herself what it was that attracted them to each other, besides the obvious. Maybe Sam was right. Maybe it was time they had "the talk," time she finally examined her feelings for him.

Only Mrs. Walker had suddenly snatched her Sunday plans from her. She had no choice but to get into her little Volkswagen Beetle and make the trek to O'Hara's Tara, the upscale condominium in downtown Atlanta where her dear friend Emma Walker lived. Obviously, something was terribly wrong.

* * *

"More coffee?" Mrs. Walker offered to pour from the silver pot. She'd set the dining table with china, crystal, and sterling.

Jennifer glared at the little woman out of the corner of her eye, and pushed what was left of her scrambled eggs into the remaining cheese grits. Breakfast was delicious down to the fresh fruit and homemade honey biscuits, but Mrs. Walker was still refusing to reveal why she'd insisted that Jennifer drop everything and speed to Atlanta.

At least the smell of food had finally enticed Tiger to abandon her. The hairless little beast loved to chew leather — even imitation leather — and didn't at all mind catching a little flesh as he tried to devour the shoe right off her foot, a point that somehow totally escaped his owner. Now he was doing a "pretty sit" in hopes of getting what was left of breakfast. Too bad he didn't know how to play dead.

"I've had two cups of coffee and more breakfast than I eat in a week. It's time you told me. . . ." Jennifer began, rubbing her sore ankle. Those scratches had better not scar.

"Uh, uh, uh. Not a word until you've

finished every bite. You'll need your strength for what lies ahead, and, knowing you, it's hard to say when you'll have your next decent meal. Just look how thin you are! You must be in the middle of one of your books and forgetting to eat. I wish I could get you to try this country ham."

Okay, enough. Mrs. Walker knew full well that Jennifer was a vegetarian. The woman was stalling, which made no sense whatsoever. Jennifer drew herself up, put down her fork, and looked her dead in the eye. "I'm done."

Mrs. Walker tossed Tiger a slice of ham almost as big as he was. He caught it in midair and crashed to the floor, growling and snarling in devilish delight.

Then Mrs. Walker faced Jennifer, her white hair framing her face angelically, her eyes large and near tears. "I don't suppose I can put it off a moment longer."

"Not and still have me around to hear about it," Jennifer assured her.

"All right then."

Jennifer wiped her hands on her cloth napkin and took the section of newspaper that Mrs. Walker handed her. It was a copy of that morning's edition of the *Atlanta Constitution*, and it was folded open to an engagement announcement.

A familiar grin stared out at her from the grainy photo. It looked like Sam — her Sam — but that was ridiculous. She leaned in closer. The hair was a little too long, and the man looked way too young, almost boyish, but that cocky attitude was right there, beaming happily out at her, his arm tight around some good-looking woman wearing a slinky evening gown, the announcement directly beneath. Some other lucky girl must have found a duplicate.

Or had she?

Her breath caught in her throat and something akin to terror grabbed her heart. *RENARD-CULPEPPER* shouted at her from the page. Obviously one of Sam's relatives . . . She scanned the article.

. . . announce the engagement of Isabelle Jean Renard of Atlanta . . . to Samuel A. Culpepper . . . graduate of the School of Journalism, the University of North Carolina, Chapel Hill, formerly of Winston-Salem, currently of Macon.

What the hell was going on?

"Oh, dear," Mrs. Walker gasped. "You've turned quite pale. I knew you'd be upset, but I didn't know any other way to break the news. You need to be with a friend when you receive information like this, a friend who has a few ideas as to how to rectify the situation."

"There must be some mistake," Jennifer insisted.

"I hardly think so. One doesn't accidently hand in the wrong names or photo for an announcement to a newspaper."

"I'm telling you, Sam is not engaged."

"You poor thing. Denial is often the first reaction. I remember when my husband Edgar first took up with —"

Jennifer pushed back from the table and stood up. "Sam is not engaged. He . . . last night . . . we . . ."

"I know, dear. Men do dissemble so." Mrs. Walker stood and wrapped her arms around Jennifer's waist. "It's all right to cry. Cry your eyes out. And when you're finished, we'll put together our plot to get him back."

Jennifer drew away, blinking back tears and swallowing the lump in her throat. Pride was as much a part of her being as her name. If Sam were engaged to some other woman, if that's what he'd been trying so hard to tell her last night, then she wanted nothing more to do with him. But she'd learned long ago that someone can't have feelings for you one moment and then suddenly not.

This was her Sam, who, just last night, had whispered in her ear how much he adored her, and who had almost said the *L* word before she placed her fingers over his lips and sent him away from her door.

How *could* he? *Why* would he?

Jennifer willed her breathing to slow, demanding that all doubt, both within herself and that directed at Sam, be put on hold. She knew this man, not thought she knew him. He had seen her through troubles that would have shaken a lesser man. He might be irritatingly candid, almost too perceptive, and have a habit of saying one more word than he should, but his integrity was beyond question. He didn't lie. He didn't deceive even when she wanted him to. She couldn't have been that wrong about him. She owed it to him to believe in him.

And until he told her otherwise, she had to assume that something about that engagement announcement was terribly wrong.

"I've got to go," Jennifer said.

"But, dear, we need to work on the plan."

"Not yet we don't." She grabbed her purse and headed for the door.

"I've already put out some feelers to find out exactly who this Isabelle person is. Actually I've hired —"

"I don't care who she is."

"Where are you going?" Mrs. Walker asked.

"To find Sam."

"But that's so . . . so direct. Do you really think it's wise?"

Wise or not, she didn't intend to take anyone else's word for it. Sam would have to tell her to her face. Was he engaged to Isabelle Jean Renard? Or not?

Chapter 4

But where the heck was Sam? He didn't answer his door or his home or cell phone no matter how many times Jennifer knocked or called. And his pager was either turned off or somewhere out of the service area. Her sympathy and understanding were under strain.

He — and his car — had disappeared off the face of the earth, or at least out of Bibb County, as best she could tell after spending hours driving past every place she thought he could possibly be. And he hadn't even called her, not even to break their afternoon date.

Mrs. Walker was right: something was terribly wrong.

Emotionally and physically exhausted, she reluctantly turned her little Beetle toward home, the light of late afternoon definitely on the wane. Twenty minutes later, she pulled into a parking space.

She climbed out of her car and headed toward the steps to her apartment building. Planted squarely in the middle of the third concrete step, shivering in a coat too thin for the weather, sat a young woman with thick, dark hair and cheeks rosy from the cold. She didn't appear to be more than seventeen, if that. Jennifer wondered how long she'd been sitting there. She squinted at the girl, who hadn't taken her eyes off Jennifer since she got out of her car. The young woman looked somehow familiar, but why? Must be a new tenant, Jennifer thought, although she couldn't remember anyone moving in or out recently.

When she came within five feet of the steps, the girl stood. "Are you Jennifer Marsh?" she asked.

Jennifer nodded. She had no time or patience to be hit up for some magazine subscription.

"I'm Suzie Turner." The girl offered her gloved hand. "I'm Suzanne Gray's niece."

Suzanne's niece? What the heck was Suzie Turner, of all people, doing on her doorstep?

That explained why she looked familiar. The family resemblance from the photos of Suzanne on TV and in the newspaper was remarkable.

"I'm sorry to bother you, Miss Marsh, but I can't find Sam Culpepper."

Surprise, surprise.

"How'd you wind up here?" Jennifer asked.

"I tried to get his address, but it's not listed anywhere, and Mom wouldn't give me his phone number. Finally I remembered that he'd written several articles about you solving crimes, and I knew you'd know how to get in touch with him. And maybe, you could help me, too. Like you have other people. I found your address in the phone book, but it didn't list which apartment you live in, only the street number. I figured you had to come in or out eventually."

"You must be Marjorie Turner's daughter."

"That's right. I can't believe you know who I am."

"Sam mentioned your mother to me. Why do you need to see him?"

"Then you do work with him sometimes," the girl said.

In truth it was more like Jennifer involving herself in situations she shouldn't, with Sam helping out in self-defense. But working together did have a better ring to it.

"Sure. What do you need?"

The girl drew a deep breath. "No one will listen. Mama says Aunt Suzanne had a dark side that I don't know anything about, and we should leave it at that. Our minister at church said Aunt Suzanne is with God now and I should be at peace with her death. And everybody else I try to talk to ignores me. The police told me they were sorry about my loss and sent me home.

"My mother says Mr. Culpepper is a good man. I know if he prints it in the newspaper, they'll have to listen to him."

"What is it you want him to print?"

"The truth. That my Aunt Suzanne didn't kill herself."

Two hot chocolates later, Jennifer had Suzie Turner warmed up enough that her teeth had stopped chattering, as much from nervous energy as from the cold, and she'd finally pulled off her coat. They sat across from each other at Jennifer's dining table, Muffy lying between their feet. Jennifer had offered to make her a sandwich, but Suzie wouldn't hear of it. She wasn't there to impose.

"How old are you?" Jennifer asked.

"Twenty-one."

Jennifer's eyebrow arched. "I thought you were younger."

"I get that all the time. I get carded every time I buy alcohol, not that I do that very often. Or go to an R-rated movie, I think it's because I have a soft voice."

And because she was polite. And open to possibilities.

"I'm sorry, but I don't know where Sam is. I can leave him a message if you want." Along with the half dozen or so she'd already recorded on his answering machine.

Her own machine hadn't had a single message on it. Sam remained MIA. Or was that AWOL?

"No, that's okay. I think I'd rather talk to you, if you don't mind. I mean, he's this big newspaper guy. I see his byline all the time. I'm not sure what I should say to him, Miss Marsh, and you're just . . . well, just a regular person."

Right. And, for once, that might actually be an advantage. As she'd told Sam, he needed her help — of course, that was assuming she ever saw him again. "Shoot. Only call me Jennifer. You're making me feel ancient."

"Okay. I know Aunt Suzanne loved Mr. Hovey, but I just don't think she would have killed herself over him. She'd been in love lots of times before."

"She told you?"

"Oh, yeah. She had tons of pictures of her old boyfriends in a box in her front closet. I know Mr. Hovey's death upset her terribly. She couldn't eat, she couldn't sleep. She wouldn't hardly talk to me, but I know she wouldn't do what she did, not without . . ."

"You two were close?"

"Mama gave me her name. And she lived with us up until I was eleven. She used to baby-sit for me when I was little. My mom's much older. There's a lot she doesn't understand. Aunt Suzanne was more like an older sister to me than an aunt. She helped me get through my teen years. I guess she was a little odd, like Mom says, but when she loved you, she loved you with her whole heart. And she did love me. I was going to be one of her bridesmaids."

"So you knew Richard Hovey."

"No. I hadn't met him yet. I work nights and that's when the two of them went out."

"But he treated her well."

"Oh, yeah. He was great."

"And you know this because . . ."

"She was always telling me about the nice things he did for her."

"Like what?"

Suzie shrugged. "Look, I know she was crushed, but you have to believe me. She wouldn't kill herself and not at least say good-bye." And for the first time, tears started down the girl's cheeks.

"Suzie, people who commit suicide, the ones who don't want to be stopped, don't tell anyone what they've got planned," Jennifer said softly, playing devil's advocate. She grabbed a napkin and handed it to Suzie who dabbed at her eyes.

"I understand that, but I know she would have left me a letter, something. But it's not even just that."

"Yes?"

"Aunt Suzanne was afraid."

"Of what?"

"Dying."

"How do you know?"

"The last time I saw her was down at her house. She hugged me to her so tight I could hardly breathe. I asked her what was wrong, and she said, 'Suzie, are you afraid to meet God?' I shook my head even though I am because I didn't know what she was getting at and I know you're not supposed to be afraid. Then she said, 'Do you think He forgives all of our sins if we ask Him to?' I told her yes because that's what she's always told me and that's what they teach us in church, but I could tell she wasn't convinced. She looked really upset, but a different upset from crying her heart out over someone that she loved. Like I said, she seemed scared. I can't bear to think of her dying like that, dying afraid."

"Lots of people are scared to die, Suzie, but that doesn't keep them from killing themselves. Some are more afraid of living."

"No, when I say she was scared, I don't mean of something in the future. I mean of something right then."

"Do you think someone was threatening your aunt?"

The girl dropped her gaze, and Muffy whimpered, snuffled at the girl's side, and laid her head in her lap. Suzie hugged the dog to her and looked up. "I don't know what else it could have been. I've never seen anyone old like that so shaken up. You've got to believe me, Jennifer. Aunt Suzanne told me flat out she didn't want to die, and you've got to help me prove it."

Chapter 5

Jennifer fed Suzie a grilled cheese sandwich and a bowl of cream of tomato soup and then sent her home with a promise to be in touch Monday, as soon as she'd found Sam. *If* she found Sam. Now she knew exactly how he'd felt in the restaurant when she'd insisted Suzanne's death wasn't suicide: helpless and at a loss to know exactly where to begin. Suspicion with no evidence of foul play led just about nowhere.

She turned on her computer and tried to write, but all she could manage was to stare at the screen. Right or not, Suzie Turner needed help. She'd turned her grief over her aunt's death into a quest for truth instead of dealing with her loss.

And Jennifer had tried to turn her worry over Sam into a need to tell him about Suzie Turner. Hah! As if that could work.

She finally fell asleep that night, her stomach in knots, listening for the phone, wondering if she could have been so thoroughly fooled by Sam and his feelings for her. She could have been more open, both with Sam and herself, about her emotions. And if she felt she had so much to prove about her writing ability, why had it seemed so necessary to deny him that journey to her success? Sam believed enough in her writing to let her work with him. Shouldn't that be enough?

But it hadn't just been her. Sam stayed so busy with work that she hadn't seen him regularly for some time. And if he hadn't had time to see her, when could he possibly have seen someone. . . .

Oh. Maybe he hadn't been quite so busy at work after all. And maybe when she'd stopped him from talking Saturday night, it hadn't been the *L* word he wanted to say. Maybe he'd been about to make one more attempt to tell her about Isabelle Renard.

It was a long night that had very little to do with sleep. By the following morning, her self-esteem had taken a nosedive.

She waited until nine o'clock and called the *Telegraph* offices. She was told that Sam hadn't made it in to work yet, that he already had a pile of messages waiting for him, and that no one had heard from him. Jennifer decided that she'd give him one more chance, but he'd better be home this time. She wouldn't seek him out again.

Hurt was giving way to anger. If he didn't want to talk to her . . .

She noted that his car was in the parking lot of his apartment building as she climbed the steps to his place in Macon's historic district. She raised her hand to knock. Did she really want to do this? Of course she did. Suzie Turner was depending on her.

She barely tapped the door before Sam flung it open. He'd obviously just gotten out of bed. She looked him up and down. His dark hair was a mess, and he had on jeans and a chambray shirt that he hadn't yet buttoned. He wore dress clothes to work, so he must not be going in today.

"So you're all right," she said. "I thought maybe you were lying dead in a ditch somewhere."

"Jennifer." Her name sounded foreign on his tongue, or maybe that was only her imagination. He gave her a puzzled frown. "Of course I'm all right. Why would you think —"

"Good. I just . . . I tried to call, but . . ." Would it kill him to jump in and help her out just a little? "Someone came by my place to see me yesterday —"

"This really isn't a good time." He

hastily buttoned his shirt and then took her elbow. "What if I call you —"

"Pepper?" The voice was lilting. Jennifer had never actually heard a voice lilt before, although she'd written it enough times in her novels. So that's what the word meant: seductively inviting. It was coming from the direction of the bedroom — the *only* bedroom in Sam's apartment.

Jennifer stopped dead. She wasn't going anywhere.

"Pepper," the voice called again, saucy this time as befitted the word. "I couldn't find any conditioner. Don't you have any?"

"Pepper?" Jennifer repeated.

Sam squinted at her. "This doesn't look good, does it?"

She squinted back. He was right about that.

A slender, long-necked woman emerged from the hallway wearing a towel around her head and Sam's terry-cloth robe. She stopped, apparently startled at seeing Jennifer standing there. She looked Jennifer up and down, then smiled a breathtaking smile and clutched the robe tightly across her chest. More modest around Jennifer than Sam it seemed.

"I didn't hear the door," she said.

Jennifer stared at her. She thought she

was the woman from the newspaper, but Jennifer wanted to be sure. She, too, looked older than the photo. “Isabelle?”

“Just Belle.”

“Right.” Jennifer took one last look at Sam’s stunned expression. “Have a nice life.”

Then she turned and walked rapidly away.

He came after her, but she was faster. She got to her car first, jumped in, locked all the doors, and backed out with Sam pounding on the windows and shouting something at her. She couldn’t hear a word, her heart was thumping so loudly in her ears. Then she floored the gas pedal and putted out of the parking lot as fast as her little Beetle would take her, hoping that the thump she heard wasn’t her tire running over his foot.

Chapter 6

Drat it all! Where could she go? If she went back to her apartment, Sam would find her there, assuming he was looking. But she wasn't yet ready to hear what he had to say about Belle, engagements, or her misinterpretation of their own relationship. She'd noticed the lack of a ring on Belle's finger, but the woman was steamy from a shower, if nothing else. She could well have taken the ring off.

Jennifer had wasted a good part of yesterday and all of last night fretting over a man who obviously hadn't been thinking about her, and, damn it, she wasn't about to allow him to rob her of another day. She swatted at the tears spilling from the corners of her eyes and tried to stay focused on the road.

What had Saturday night been about? What kind of game was Sam playing? Had he planned to fill her with wine, sweep her onto the dance floor, and then mention between nibbles to her earlobe, "Oh, by the way, I have a fiancée"?

And what the heck was all that talk about their writing a book together? Not in this lifetime. Besides, Sam had other things on his mind at the moment, while she didn't. In fact, she had all the time in the world now that he was out of the picture.

But Suzanne Gray had a story that begged to be told, a story about love gone bad, a woman's story, one that her niece desperately wanted unraveled. There was no law saying Jennifer couldn't write a book all by herself. She was certainly capable of it, and she needed a distraction in the worst way.

Suzanne — foolish woman — had died, whether by her own hand or someone else's, over the love of one Richard Hovey. The question was why. And the best way to get a feel for exactly what had happened to poor, misguided Suzanne was to visit the scene of her death.

Bibb Memorial Gardens looked deserted as her little Volkswagen Bug chugged through the old brick archway and over the narrow, winding road that snaked through the property. No wonder no one was out to pay their respects. It was as cold a Monday morning as she could remember, and her car's pathetic excuse for a heater was making far more noise than heat. She shivered — whether from anger or from cold, it was impossible to tell — as she shifted into second gear and headed slowly up the little hill.

Richard hadn't been buried long enough — less than a week — for a grave marker to be erected, but a fresh grave has a telltale mound of earth that takes months to settle. She passed one covered by a green canopy and heaps of cut flowers. Too fresh. But further up the hill, in the back section, she spotted a site near a large pine tree, maybe forty feet from the road.

She stopped the car, pulled on the emergency brake, and got out. Darn it was cold, a settle-down-into-your-bones cold, and the wind was fierce, chapping her cheeks where her tears had fallen. There was no sun, just a gray sky, a perfect fit for her mood.

She found her way to the mound, careful not to step on any graves. The least one could do for the dead was to respect their space.

The morning dew had frozen into ice crystals that clung to the grass. They crunched under her feet and dotted the plastic flower arrangements adorning most of the graves. Not even a single carnation was left to mourn this person's passing. Maybe the police had cleared them all away. Or the groundskeeper who'd found poor Suzanne, who had thrown herself away for some man who would never know the sacrifice she'd made.

How had she felt, lying on that heap of earth, the cold creeping gradually into her flesh, numbing first her back, fingers and toes, and then robbing her calves and forearms of all sensation, while the ironic strains of the Beatles in the background promised love as the solution to her problems? Love she could no longer have. Love that was as dead as she was soon to be. Love that was only an illusion.

Or had she been too out of it with pills to have felt anything? But she couldn't have been and still set up the scene.

Why had she done such a thing to herself? Why hadn't she taken the pills and lain down in the comfort of her own warm bed, a photo of Richard clutched to her chest? Why hadn't she simply gone to join her love in her dreams? Why hadn't she signed that blasted suicide note?

Because she hadn't killed herself, Jennifer concluded. Not that way. It just didn't make sense.

Jennifer looked toward the road. Where

had they found her car? It had to have been parked nearby.

"A little cold for you to be out here."

The voice startled her and she turned. "You shouldn't sneak up on a person like that. You could have given me a heart attack."

The man grinned at her. His skin was dark and his upper lip sported a black mustache. He wore rumpled green work clothes, a thick jacket open down the front, worn-out brown boots, and a baseball cap that was pulled tight over his curly hair. "Well, now, I guess this is the place to have one. Eliminates the extra trip. 'Sides, I wasn't sneakin' nowhere. You were lost in your thoughts. You related to this one?" He pointed at the mound.

"No. I don't even know who's buried here. I was looking for Richard Hovey's grave."

"Hey, you all right?"

"Sure. Why?"

"Your eyes. They're all red."

"Yeah, well, the wind makes them sting. Is this Hovey?"

"Nah. He's back over near the crypt. C'mon, I'll show you."

She followed him as he led her across the gently rolling hillside. She noticed he didn't mind stepping on graves, but then if he did mind, she couldn't imagine how he'd ever get any work done.

"Here," he said. "It's not easy buryin' them when the ground's cold like this."

This mound was more settled than the one before, perhaps because of all the police and news reporters tromping over it. The area looked as though it had been swept clean, yet one single red rose remained. "Thanks," Jennifer said.

"Hey, no problem."

The man seemed reluctant to leave, which was just as well because she didn't intend to let him get away, at least not before she'd asked him a question. "Were you the one who found Suzanne Gray?"

"You a reporter?"

"Nope."

"Police?"

"Do I look like a police officer?" Jennifer tried to smile.

"Can't tell by looks since they took away all those macho requirements, but I figure you'd be flashin' a badge at me if you were. You weren't sweet on this guy, were you?" He grinned at her, but his eyes were serious, no doubt taking in the streaks her tears had left in her makeup. One suicide was probably more than the place needed.

She shook her head. "I read about it in the newspaper. It just seems so sad." She let out a loud sniff and choked back more tears. It really was sad. Love was sad.

"Women! You can call it whatever you want, but I call it just plain stupid." He bent and picked up the rose. "Why you all come up here and visit some dead man —"

"Who's come up here?"

"I don't know, but I keep findin' these roses left here."

Jennifer cleared her throat. "How many?"

"One each day since the funeral."

"Do you mind?" She put out her hand and he handed her the rose. The thorns had been removed. High quality. This one hadn't come from any grocery store.

"You found her, didn't you?" Jennifer asked.

"On my mornin' rounds. Good God o'mighty I don't ever wanna see a sight like what I saw that mornin'."

"What did you see?"

He hesitated.

"No, really. You can tell me."

"And why's that?"

"Because . . . because I don't have anyone to tell." At least not yet. And if she ever did write a book about Suzanne, she'd ask his permission first.

"I guess that's fair." He paused for a moment, staring toward the Ocmulgee River, but Jennifer felt certain he wasn't seeing the landscape. "She looked like a great big china doll lyin' there, laid out so fine, surrounded by all those flowers, her dark hair spread all around her head, wearin' a plain white summer dress. Her lips were real blue-like. Her eyes closed like she was sleepin'. Her eyebrows and eyelashes, her hair, too, were frosted like sugar had been sprinkled all over her. Still. Not a breath. Not a movement. I touched her just to make sure. Didn't need no doctor to tell me she was dead. I see dead people all the time, but I never seen one frozen stiff like that."

"What kind of security do you have working here at night?"

"Don't really have any. The police drive through every now and again. I've been workin' here fourteen years, and we haven't had no more than a couple of tipped gravestones in all that time. Kids. That was over in the old section. They don't allow nothin' but these flat markers these days."

"Did you find anything not mentioned in the newspaper?"

He shook his head. "Nothin' but the body, the cloth, the tape player, and the flowers she was holdin'. The police found an empty Southern Comfort bottle tossed behind that tree over there. It wasn't there the day before. I keep this place clean."

If the cold hadn't gotten her, the combination of pills and alcohol would have.

"How about her car?" Jennifer asked.

"It was back over there a ways." He pointed toward the direction they'd come from. "I noticed it when I come in to work but didn't think nothin' of it. People come here all hours, but most of them who drive leave on their own."

"When will the marker go up?" she asked.

"Most likely not for another month."

Jennifer nodded. "You mind if I stay a little longer?"

"Do what you want. We're open to the public."

He took the hint and headed down toward the crypt. When he got there he turned back and looked at her before going off.

She offered a little wave. It was nice that he cared, even if it was only because he didn't want to explain one more frozen corpse to his boss. Then she bent down and touched the red earth. Dust to dust. She wasn't sure what she'd expected to find at Hovey's grave. She was certain the police had scoured every inch. If anything had been left, it'd probably been trampled into the earth.

"Richard," she said aloud. Talking to the dead didn't seem odd to her. She often spoke to her parents, but so far they'd never answered her. "Tell me, would Suzanne actually have killed herself over you? And why would some other woman care so much that she'd brave the cold to visit you every morning? What kind of hold did you have over them?"

The wind picked up, whistling at her head and tearing at the flower in her hand, whipping off two petals. "Well, if you won't tell me, I guess I'll just have to find out for myself who your mystery woman is. You, me, and your lady have an appointment. Bright and early tomorrow morning."

Chapter 7

But morning and Jennifer's appointment with Richard's "lady" were a long while off. She grabbed a salad at a fast-food restaurant, ate it in her car, and punched in Suzie's number on her cell phone. The girl worked the evening shift at the Starvin' Marvin not too far from her house, and, as she'd told Jennifer, close enough that her mother could be at the store in five minutes if she ever ran into any trouble. It was two-thirty. The phone rang twice before a soft voice answered hello. She sounded so young, so vulnerable over the phone.

"Suzie, it's Jennifer. I found Sam, but he's . . . pretty busy at the moment. I think we should go ahead without him. I'm headed for the library, the main one, downtown. Want to meet me there?" She heard Suzie yawn. "Did I wake you?"

"No, it's all right. I was late getting in from work last night. I lay back down for a nap after breakfast. I'll throw something on, grab a banana, and be there in about thirty minutes. I'll have to slip out the front, so Mom won't stop me and try to feed me lunch."

"Okay. See you then." Jennifer cranked up her car and headed uptown to one of the best sources of information she knew of, the Bibb County Library. It was located in a large white building not all that far from Sam's apartment in the old part of Macon. Sam would never think to look for her there, almost on his doorstep, and a lot of what had been written about Richard Hovey and Suzanne Gray was most likely right on the shelves or in the microfiche housed in the old building's toasty warmth. She could even check the Internet without going home.

Jennifer remembered a big article about Hovey the day after he died. She flipped through the stack of back issues of the *Telegraph*, and there was his photo right on the front page with the headline: *NATIONALLY KNOWN MACON ATTORNEY RICHARD HOVEY DIES.*

A most attractive man. His hair was still dark with just a hint of silver around his temples. His nose was long, his jaw angular, his eyes large, dark, and brooding under thick eyebrows. His physique was still slender. He had the poise of a man who wore an expensive suit as though it was his due.

But there was something about his looks that she didn't trust. Beneath his veneer of seductive sincerity was an invitation to danger. He looked like someone who didn't like to lose, wouldn't tolerate it. Did Suzanne have any idea what kind of fire she'd been playing with?

Renowned attorney Richard Foster Hovey, 42, . . .

Funny how, in death, "shady" became "renowned." But wasn't the law a numbers game, just like everything else? Wins versus losses. Very little else mattered.

. . . was found dead at his home on Oglethorpe Street January 31, the victim of a fall.

Short and to the point. No mention of rose petals.

Mr. Hovey is probably best known for his defense of mass murderer Abraham Eckel . . .

Hovey should have been jailed for that

one. Anyone who used a technicality to get off a mass murderer who planned to kill again . . . Thank God the police had caught him before he managed one more victim.

. . . and his most recent work for alleged wife killer Simon DeSoto. Mr. Hovey, sought as a consultant on cases all over the nation, had a reputation for winning acquittals for clients who had little hope of success. His arguments before the state supreme court are often cited.

A fairly in-depth recounting of the DeSoto case and conviction followed, including the fact that Hovey had filed a petition to have the verdict set aside.

And it had been. By a judge who might as well hang up his career. He'd ensured his defeat in the next election, even if he had been following the letter of the law.

She flipped to the inside of the B section where a conventional obit added the following information:

Survivors include his former wife, Mrs. Ruth Loudermilk Hovey; a son, Darrell Hovey; two daughters, Melanie Hovey and Mrs. Virginia Hovey Boyd; and his par-

ents, Mr. and Mrs. Oliver Hovey.

So, the ex-Mrs. Hovey was a Loudermilk. They had money. Owned a good amount of land on the east side of Macon, just past the city limits, if Jennifer remembered correctly. Ruth Hovey had to be part of that family. And it would make all kinds of sense for Hovey to have formed that union, as ambitious as he obviously was. The fact that one of their daughters was already married suggested the Hoveys had wed young. Hell hath no fury like a woman who puts her husband through law school — with or without the aid of her family's money — and then gets dumped.

> *Funeral services will be conducted at 11 A.M. today at Bibb Memorial Gardens. The family requests that donations be made to charity in lieu of flowers.*

No mention of Suzanne Gray. Or any other significant other. She wondered if Suzanne had attended his funeral. And, if so, how the ex-Mrs. Hovey felt about her being there. Suzie should know.

One day later, Suzanne was dead herself. What had that day been like for her? Hell, most likely. Ignored, excluded. Could she have been so distraught that she typed that note and forgot to sign it above her typed name? Typed name. That still didn't make sense.

And what about Ruth? Was she devastated by Richard's death? Was she embarrassed by Suzanne's? The latter was a given. Who wouldn't be?

Jennifer folded the copy of the *Telegraph* and returned it to its shelf. Then she found the edition with Sam's article across the front page. A smiling Suzanne stared from a studio photo, crinkles around her eyes, as though she had no cares in the world, her hair dark and full, chin length. She looked young for her age, Jennifer thought, like an older version of Suzie. Pleasant enough, but not particularly attractive while Suzie was actually quite pretty. Of course youth in itself holds a lot of appeal.

She scanned down through the article to see if there was anything she'd missed.

. . . local businesswoman . . . O Happy Day Delivery Service, a balloon/candy/flowers/singing gram service co-owned by Kelli Byers . . . graduate of Sherwood High School.

No college mentioned.

Sam had done well by her. He had set

the scene and explained the facts of her death, but he didn't exploit them. He left her dignity intact.

Jennifer shuffled through the B section of the paper. Photos of lovely brides and smiling grooms caught her eye and her stomach gave a lurch. The pain she'd pushed away so hard was again gripping her chest.

Sam, how could you? I thought you had more class. All I've ever asked from you is honesty.

Tears were threatening again, but she refused to cry. Not here. Not in a public place. She pulled a tissue out of her purse and dabbed at her nose.

Someone called her name.

"I got here as fast as I could," Suzie told her, sliding into the chair next to her. She'd thrown on an old Sherwood High School sweatshirt and some jeans. Then she looked Jennifer full in the face. "What's wrong?"

"Nothing." Jennifer sniffed and blinked hard. "I think I'm catching a cold. It's trying to go to my eyes."

"We'll all be sick with flu if this weather doesn't break soon. I don't ever remember cold like this lasting so long."

"Neither do I. Suzie, did your aunt attend Hovey's funeral?"

"I don't know. I didn't see her all that day. He was buried the morning of the day she . . ."

"Right." Suzanne had died that night, the same day as Hovey's funeral.

She started to fold the paper when Suzie tapped the lower left-hand corner, and a headline leaped. *GRAY-HOVEY TO WED.* There it was. In the very same newspaper that carried news of Suzanne's death was her engagement announcement to a dead Richard Hovey.

"They were getting married in June," Suzie said.

"She told you about it."

"Of course. I was going to be her bridesmaid. She talked about it all the time. She really loved him."

"But you still don't think she killed herself."

Suzie shook her head. "Men were always falling in love with Aunt Suzanne. Even our minister had a little something for her, but I wouldn't breathe that to anybody but you. She had to know she'd find someone else, even if it took a long time to get over Mr. Hovey. They had only known each other a few months. There's always someone else out there for us, isn't there? If love goes wrong? That's what Aunt Suzanne always told me."

She should have Suzie talk to her writers' group, explain to them that being thirty and unmarried didn't mean she'd never find someone else. Maybe not another Sam, but . . . she sniffed hard. Better to keep her thoughts on Suzanne.

"And you don't think Hovey was seeing anyone else."

"Are you kidding?" Suzie asked. "He was dating my Aunt Suzanne."

Okay. So Jennifer didn't know that was supposed to be a stupid question.

"She had this almost magical appeal," Suzie explained. "She wasn't like the rest of us — not like you and me. Men were drawn to her."

Jennifer stole a look at Suzie. The kid was serious. And maybe she was right. A touch, a look, a hidden promise — a woman didn't have to be conventionally pretty to be amazingly sexy.

Jennifer put the newspaper back on its rack in the reserve room. "Come on, let's check the Internet."

The two of them found an empty carrel in the computer room, and with Suzie looking over her shoulder, she logged on and brought up a search engine. She typed in *Richard Hovey* and got so many hits, she didn't know where to start.

"Wow! I know Aunt Suzanne said he was well known, but I had no idea."

Even Jennifer was surprised. Hovey's name popped up in articles from the *New York Times* to the *Washington Post* and the *Philadelphia Inquirer.* He'd been called in as a consultant on all kinds of trials across the country.

They scanned the titles of as many articles as they could, knowing that they could retrieve all that information later. Right now what Jennifer was really interested in was Hovey's relationship with Suzanne.

"Have you ever tried searching for your aunt's name?"

Suzie shook her head. "I don't have a computer. Kelli does. Aunt Suzanne's partner. I think they have a Web site, but I've never seen it."

Jennifer entered Suzanne's name into the search engine and got dozens of hits, all from newspaper articles about her death. And one hit for O Happy Day Delivery Service. She clicked on the link and the computer came alive. Balloons of red, blue, and yellow swelled across the screen and then exploded, showering confetti over the name of the service, which was surrounded by pictures of cut flowers and wrapped candies. She could tell by the way the flowers danced that if speakers had been connected, music would be playing. Such a happy display.

"Would you look at that! That's neat!" Suzie said.

Jennifer grinned. It was indeed neat. And just as one more balloon filled and then popped, she had a thought.

"You say your aunt didn't have a computer. How about a typewriter?"

"No. But she could use Kelli's anytime she wanted. She lives just across the road."

Which meant that Suzanne didn't have anything convenient to type a suicide note on. Unless she'd used Kelli's machine, which would make her the accomplice. Why hadn't Sam checked that out?

"Kelli's kind of weird," Suzie went on, "but she does know her computer stuff. She does all the advertisements for the business."

"Weird how?"

"Oh, you know." Suzie shrugged. "I just don't much like her. I always thought she was jealous of Aunt Suzanne."

"How so?"

"Well, because Aunt Suzanne got so much attention, you know, and Kelli didn't like other people around Aunt Suzanne. If Aunt Suzanne and I went to the movies, we'd have to slip out if we didn't want Kelli to come, too."

Jennifer jotted down the phone number at the bottom of the screen. Kelli Byers was most likely still running the business. And anyone who was jealous of Suzanne Gray was someone she wanted to speak with. Then she returned to the search engine and typed in *Ruth Loudermilk Hovey.*

"Why do you want to know about Mr. Hovey's ex-wife?" Suzie asked.

"Suzie, if your aunt didn't kill herself, someone had to do it."

"But you can't think his wife . . ."

"I don't think anything. I'm just putting her name into the computer to see what comes up."

Ruth's name appeared on three links. One had to do with the Cherry Blossom Festival. Of course she'd be involved with that. The next concerned the Macon Woman's Club. But the last was something else entirely, a gossip column from the *Atlanta Eye* dated two years ago.

RUTH HOVEY CHARTS HUSBAND'S SUCCESS

The buzz around the Bibb County

Courthouse is that the key to Richard Hovey's phenomenal success in the courtroom is Ruth Hovey's personal astrologer. Ruth is reported to employ the astrologer, a la Nancy Reagan, to schedule Richard's court appearances. Does it work? This reporter can only say it obviously doesn't hurt.

"She's a nut," Suzie pronounced. "No wonder her husband left her."

"Maybe, maybe not," Jennifer said. Had Ruth been trying to influence her husband or was this a desperate attempt to be more a part of his life? How did Richard view her little hobby? She hardly thought he'd be pleased that a tabloid had attributed his success to an astrologer. And who, Jennifer wondered, did she consult when her marriage hit the rocks?

Or was the story simply not true? One of the basic tenets of journalism was consider your source: the *Atlanta Eye*.

Her stomach growled and she turned off the computer. That salad hadn't been much, but a vegetarian had only so many fast-food options.

"I'm hungry. How about you?" she asked Suzie.

"Starved. All I've had all day is a banana, a Coke, and a cold piece of pizza for breakfast."

"What do you say we grab an early dinner?"

"Sounds good. My shift starts at seven."

Jennifer dug her cell phone out of her purse. If she was hungry, that meant Muffy was, too. The dog was no doubt pouting from her absence. She'd also need to be walked.

The voice of her neighbor, Mrs. Ramon, came on the line, her thick accent even more difficult to understand with the chaos of children in the background.

"Mrs. Ramon —"

"Jennifer, you get yourself back here pronto. That fellow of yours has come knocking on your door twice now and then mine. I told him I know not where you are, but he seems really upset. What you done now, *mi chica?*"

"Could you please ask one of the kids to feed Muffy and take her out for her walk? Her leash is in the closet. And ask them to give her a treat. There's a box on top of the refrigerator. But only one treat. She has to watch her weight."

"Of course. I do whatever I can for you. You know that. But what has happened? Your young man —"

"It's all right. I'll take care of it."

"No, Miss Jennifer. You get your head out of the dirt —"

"Out of the sand," Jennifer corrected.

"Out of wherever you put it that you shouldn't have," Mrs. Ramon insisted. "Your young man have with him this woman, *muy linda*, hair like, what you say, copper. You take care, my young friend. You get yourself back here, I warn you. I don't like the look in her eye. I don't trust this one."

"I appreciate your concern but just take care of the dog. Please. I'll take care of everything else. I've got to go." She hit the phone's off button.

"What's wrong?" Suzie asked.

"Nothing." She wasn't about to tell Suzie her troubles. At least it wasn't tears that threatened this time. It was anger. Sam had brought that woman to her home. How could he?

Anger was so much easier to deal with than hurt, but, in truth, she wasn't much good dealing with either one. Maybe that's why she wrote. It gave her control. Before relationships got too complicated or messy, she could always kill off one of the people involved. That was the advantage of mystery over romance: no one was guaranteed to make it to the end. Too bad Belle Renard wasn't as easily dispensed with as the characters in her books.

"Are you sure you're all right?" Suzie asked. "You're spacing out on me."

"I'm sure. You've got to get to work and I've got to get to my writers' meeting. We'll have supper and then we can both take off. Sound good?"

"Great."

Food had again lost its appeal. Jennifer wanted a hole to crawl into. Barring that, her writers' group would simply have to do. Unfortunately, she hadn't anticipated what she'd find there, or she wouldn't have gone.

Chapter 8

When Jennifer walked into Monique's den, four sets of eyes stared at her with such I'm-so-glad-it's-you-and-not-me sadness written all over their faces. Clearly, they all knew about Sam and Isabelle Renard.

Pity. In all its ugliness. What could be worse? Nothing, except maybe seeing that wretched engagement announcement again. Monique, no doubt, subscribed to the Sunday edition of the *Atlanta Constitution.*

Jennifer pursed her lips and folded the copy of the paper waiting for her on her customary seat on Monique's sectional sofa. The cowards. Not one of them had had the courage to call her, at least not on Sunday. They'd probably spoken with each other and then hatched their plan to wait, knowing that once she came to their writers' meeting, she'd have no way to escape.

She couldn't control the redness she felt burning in her cheeks, but she sure as heck wasn't going to allow Leigh Ann, Teri,

April, Monique, or anyone else for that matter, to feel sorry for her. Or talk behind her back. There were worse things than being alone. Her Southern pride had long ago taught her that. Of course, pride wasn't much of a conversationalist, or companion, and it didn't have the deepest, darkest bluest eyes. . . .

She tossed aside the newspaper.

"You poor thing," dark-haired Leigh Ann whispered, tears welling, her petite body shuddering with emotion. "You're so brave. You've been going with Sam a good while now. I thought, well, I thought someday it'd be you in that photo with him."

"I say we kill the two-timing son of a bitch," Teri growled from her spot on the floor, her dark eyes half-lidded, a menacing determination creasing her cocoa-brown skin. "Jennifer writes the best mysteries ever written, published or not. We could lose the body where nobody could find it."

"Now, now, you don't mean that," April cautioned, her big blue eyes wide with shock. After all, she was the mother of two young children. "Violence is never a solution. But misery — and lots of mental anguish — that could be arranged."

"When did the two of you break up?" Monique asked quietly from her solid maple rocker, her plain, fortyish face earnest, reasonable. "And why didn't you tell us about it?"

Jennifer looked at them. First Monique, solid, older, obviously rationally weighing the situation; then April, plump, sweet, optimistic but ever pragmatic; Teri, protective, belligerent, definitely out for blood; and finally Leigh Ann, the true romantic of the group, who couldn't have been more crushed if she had just lost the one true love of her own life.

Jennifer took a deep breath. "We didn't. The newspaper was the first I'd heard of it."

"Oh, no. Jennifer's the other woman," Leigh Ann declared, rising up from the corner of the sectional sofa, her green eyes huge, her small mouth drawn into a disapproving bow. "He must have been dating this . . . this . . . what the heck was her name again?"

"Isabelle Jean Renard," April supplied from her seat on the other sofa.

"This Renard woman all the time he's been going with our Jennifer. I thought he was too good a catch to be single. Where did the paper say she was from?"

"Atlanta now, but her family's from North Carolina," Monique reminded them.

"Isn't that where Sam's from?" Leigh Ann asked. "They've probably known each other for years, before Jennifer and Sam even met."

"Don't any of you have anything to read?" Jennifer demanded. "The last time I looked at our bylaws, this was supposed to be a writers' group where members read their work aloud and get critical suggestions."

"Do we have bylaws?" Leigh Ann asked.

Teri nodded and stretched. "That piece of paper Monique handed out at our first meeting."

"That was years ago. Were we supposed to read it?"

Monique drew herself up. "Jennifer's right. What's going on between her and Sam is none of our business, at least not until she decides it is. Leigh Ann, I think you had something you said you wanted to read tonight, the start of a new romance novel."

Leigh Ann nodded, digging folded pages out from the bottom of her large purse. "I worked on this yesterday evening, and I thought I'd let you all give me your first impression." She glanced pointedly at Jennifer before her eyes found the typed page. Then she cleared her throat and began.

"Jenette looked over the cliffs at the dark, inviting waves crashing against the huge, polished stones below. The cold wind whipped at her hair and shawl, billowing her long skirt. But that iciness could not match the cold she felt where her heart had once been. The only warmth in her entire being was the lingering memory of Seth's kiss on her lips and the look of longing in his eyes. He loved her, loved her deep, down to her bones, down to her very marrow, and she knew it. No matter what anyone said, no matter what rumors flew about that hussy Belinda who was said to have stolen him from her. No one could take their love away, not as long as she wouldn't allow it. All she had to do was be strong, trust in him, believe in their love, follow her heart, be true to —"

"Okay," Jennifer interrupted. "I get the message."

Leigh Ann blinked. "Whatever do you mean?"

Teri rolled her eyes. "Hang it up, Leigh. She's on to you. Not that any moron wouldn't be."

"I'm not going to talk about it," Jennifer insisted. "Besides, that engagement announcement is the least of what's bothering me."

They all turned expectantly toward Jennifer. Cripes. Seems she never quite knew when to shut up. Now she had two choices. Explain or leave. Hah! As if she'd ever make it out of there.

"I saw Sam this morning."

"Well, thank the good Lord for that," April said. "And he told you —"

"And he was with Belle Renard."

That struck them all silent, at least for the moment.

"Shall we take a vote? Who's in favor of my solution?" Teri asked, raising her hand.

A loud pounding sounded on Monique's door as both Leigh Ann's and April's hands shot up. They each looked at one another. Jennifer checked her watch. It was seven-fifteen.

"Excuse me just a moment. Everyone I'm acquainted with knows not to come by here on Monday nights," Monique insisted, dragging herself out of her rocker and heading for the door.

No one said a word. They were hardly ever disturbed. As Monique said, everyone knew better. Sitting quietly, they all strained to listen as Monique opened the door to the intruder.

"I don't think that's such a good idea," Monique protested from the hallway.

A masculine voice responded. "I've been looking for her all day. I know she's here. If you don't let me in, I'll . . . I'll wait outside until she leaves."

Oh, no. It was Sam. Jennifer's perpetual blush deepened. Couldn't he at least leave her some modicum of dignity? Did he have to play out their problems in front of her dearest friends?

"All right then."

And Monique was actually going to let him in. How could she? Quickly, she scanned the room. There was nowhere to hide.

He stopped just inside the doorway to the den. He looked horrible, deep circles under those dark blue eyes of his, his hair still wild. Had he not combed it all day? Had Belle not noticed? What kind of girlfriend was she?

"We have to talk," Sam insisted. He started toward her, but Teri spread her legs across the floor in front of Jennifer. That stopped him.

"Say the word and I'll take him down," Teri offered. Her brown belt in karate would probably be enough to do just that, considering the state Sam was in. "I think I should warn you we've just had a vote —"

"Please," he begged. "It's not what it looked like. Belle is —"

"I'm not romantically involved with Pepper." That voice, spunky now, as Belle appeared at the doorway. Did she not realize that one needed an invitation to come into someone's house? But what was one more? They might as well have a convention of all the parties involved right there in Monique's den.

Jennifer threw up her hands. "Do you mind? We're having a meeting here."

"I'd say we're having quite a meeting here," Leigh Ann muttered, a delicious smile on her lips. "Pepper, huh?"

"I'll be home by nine o'clock, Sam," Jennifer stated. "Call me then."

"And risk that you might not answer your phone or show up at all? No way," he insisted.

"Why bother with me? You seem to have your future . . ." Suddenly, Jennifer sat straight up. "Did she say you're not involved romantically?"

Belle nodded her head, her soft, reddish brown curls swishing on her shoulders. She was dressed in a sweatshirt and jeans, not the most fetching outfit.

"That's what I've been trying to tell you," Sam said.

"I knew they weren't really engaged," Leigh Ann said, grinning and relaxing back against a cushion.

"But I saw the two of you . . . the bathrobe . . . the conditioner . . ." Jennifer began.

"Conditioner?" April repeated. "What kind of conditioner?"

"I found Belle in Atlanta Sunday evening and insisted she come back with me to my place."

"Oh, man, you are *not* helping your case," Teri warned.

"Do you think we could go somewhere and talk?" Sam suggested, nodding toward the door. "Without the audience."

The frying pan or the fire. Staying would only put off the inevitable and mean listening to her friends drone on about Sam and Belle, especially now that they'd seen her in the all-too-becoming flesh. She sighed and stood up. At least she had the keys to her car. Maybe she could make a getaway.

Sam tried to take her elbow, but she shrugged him off. She wasn't about to let him touch her. Quickly, she stepped over Teri's legs, grabbed her coat off a chair, and headed for the front door.

"Call me," Leigh Ann hollered after her.

Without a backward glance, Jennifer was out the door and down the steps, Sam and Belle trailing after.

"Give me your keys," Sam insisted behind her.

She turned and asked innocently, "Why?"

"Because I know you. Cough them up."

"No way."

"If you run over my other foot, I'll probably be crippled for life."

"I didn't actually hurt you, did I?"

"Only caught the tip of my shoe. All I'm asking for is one hour of your time. I think, after all we've been through together, you owe me that much."

She looked at her watch. It was seven-twenty. "One hour."

"If you still want to tell me to go to hell by —"

"Eight-twenty," she supplied.

"By eight-twenty, I'll go away and leave you alone." He opened the door to his Honda and helped her in. Belle let herself into the backseat.

"So she's coming with us," Jennifer observed.

"That's right," Sam told her. "I don't intend to let her out of my sight. Belle is in danger."

Chapter 9

"Just who," Jennifer didn't add the *besides me* she was thinking, "wants you dead?" She leaned across the table in a booth far in the back of Alfie's Diner. Belle must have someone specific in mind.

"I don't know that anyone actually wants me dead," Belle said.

"Saturday night someone broke into her apartment and went through her belongings," Sam explained. "She was just lucky she wasn't home when it happened."

"Nothing of any value was destroyed," Belle insisted.

"The place was ransacked and that's not the half of it," Sam went on.

"I told you, it was only one small death threat." Belle removed the top of her bun and slathered her hamburger with ketchup. "It's not as if I haven't had them before. Man, I'm hungry. I didn't think he was ever going to stop chasing after you long enough for us to have anything to eat. I hate that they won't serve these rare anymore." She grinned at Sam. "Remember when we used to go to that place in Durham? What was the name of it?"

"I think it was Hamburger Haven," Sam suggested.

"No, Heaven, wasn't it? Yes, I'm sure that's right," Belle said, looking at him out of the corner of her eye, a smile curving her lip.

Sam shuffled his legs under the table, and Jennifer suspected Belle had been rubbing her foot against his calf.

"If you're in such danger, why don't you just go to the police?" Jennifer snapped. She'd seen that we-have-a-past exclusionary tactic before, and she wasn't about to let Belle get away with using it. Or with playing footsie with Sam under the table. "You're going to have to explain how some bogus engagement announcement — without the groom's knowledge — offers you any kind of protection from a death threat. It obviously didn't stop someone from breaking in."

"That was poor timing on my part. I should have put it in last week," Belle said.

"You shouldn't have put it in at all," Jennifer said.

"The article in the paper was Belle's rather creative idea of insurance," Sam explained, stirring his coffee. At least he had the decency not to have an appetite.

"How so? She didn't even ask you first!" She turned to Belle. "Do you not realize he has a life? What were you thinking?"

"Hey, take a chill," Belle suggested.

Sam placed a restraining hand on Jennifer's forearm. She shook it off, but settled down next to him on the bench. Getting angry was not going to make her look good in Sam's eyes, and he was in a difficult position. After all, jealousy ranked at about the same level of hell as pity. She was loathe to admit it, but she hated Belle already, even if the woman was in danger. And it didn't help a bit that Belle sat there with her little-girl smile and perfect white teeth, her smooth skin flushed a charming peach, and with dimples to boot, while Jennifer played the enraged girlfriend. She knew how she looked when she got angry and pretty wasn't it.

And why did men love women who ate beef? Where was the attraction in that?

Belle wiped ketchup from the corner of her mouth and swallowed. "Look, I never expected Pepper to see that announcement. I doubt that a guy like him even knows the style section exists. Besides, it was in a newspaper from another city. And, of course, I didn't know about you — that he was involved with anyone. It was the only thing I could think of with such short notice." She turned toward Sam. "I would never intentionally create trouble for you. You know that, don't you?"

There it was again, that darned lilting. And that gag-me-with-a-spoon syrupy sweetness.

"You should have called first," he told her.

She gave him a glowing smile. "I'm sorry. Of course I should have, but we hadn't seen each other in over two years, and I didn't want to bother you."

"Bother him!" The words exploded from Jennifer's mouth before she could stifle them. Belle should get her own boyfriend if she needed someone to rescue her.

"Wouldn't you like something to eat?" Sam offered, shoving the shared basket of fries in her direction.

She shook her head and gave him a look out of the corner of her eye. She'd had very little of the pizza she and Suzie had ordered, but stuffing food in her mouth was more likely to make her choke than to keep her quiet. She'd try to do better.

"Who's trying to kill you?" Jennifer asked again, more softly this time.

Belle took another bite of burger. "About eighteen months ago, I did some undercover work. I'm a reporter."

"That's how you two know each other?" Jennifer asked.

"Oh, Pepper and I go way back," Belle assured her, talking and chewing at the same time. "We were both journalism majors at UNC Chapel Hill. We worked together on the college newspaper."

Just as Jennifer had figured. Late nights thinking up ways to aggravate the administration. She remembered them well. As someone once said, there's nothing sexier than fomenting revolution.

"Which newspaper do you work for?"

Belle hesitated. "The *Atlanta Eye*."

Jennifer couldn't help but let a smile escape. So *that's* why Jennifer didn't recognize her name. She refused to open that scandal rag.

"But that's only temporary," Belle hastily added. "As I started to tell you, I got involved with the Simon DeSoto murder case, managed to get close to him."

"She fooled DeSoto into thinking she was interested in him," Sam explained, his mouth drawn, obviously disgusted with Belle's foolhardiness. "We all knew he was suspected in the murder of his wife, but the police couldn't get any evidence against him."

"And the newspaper sanctioned —" Jennifer began and then stopped herself. At the *Eye*, anything went. And the people they hired . . . Well, Teague McAfee was a prime example. Young, obnoxious, persistent as a pit bull, and ready to sacrifice the truth for a good story any day.

"I read every word about that case," Jennifer went on. She kept up with all the notorious murder cases in the state of Georgia. It made for great research for her novels. "I don't remember any mention of a girlfriend."

"Right," Belle agreed. "Because I never had to testify against him. I found evidence of his contacts with the hired gun, mainly by gaining entry to his home and going through his phone bills. DeSoto never knew it was me. Once the killer was located, he copped a plea and testified against DeSoto."

"And now . . ." Light was dawning. DeSoto had been released. And he was looking for Belle. "You're crazy," Jennifer said.

"Well, it didn't seem so crazy at the time," Belle told her. "How'd I know Hovey would get the guy's verdict set aside?"

"I can't believe he was able to do that." Jennifer shook her head.

"I know," Sam agreed. "But some of the evidence is being challenged, or at least its interpretation."

"But you'd think that now Hovey is dead —"

"Doesn't matter who defends DeSoto now," Belle said. "If he can show other people were in his home, and worse yet, that he wasn't in his home when some of those phone calls were going on, he'll be home free. Reasonable doubt."

"Right," Sam agreed. "From what I was able to find out between trips to your apartment, he's got a strong case, assuming no one is perjuring himself. The theory Hovey was most recently putting forth was that the killer was hired by someone else but rolled over on DeSoto in order to make the deal."

"So DeSoto thinks you were sincere," Jennifer suggested, "that you actually cared about him." It was beginning to make some kind of twisted sense.

"I hope he still thinks that. It's better than him thinking I tried to screw him over."

"Does he know you work for the newspaper?" Jennifer asked.

"Yes, but cracking major news stories is

not the *Eye*'s usual fare. I saw this story as my way back to the legitimate press. Unfortunately, none of my work about the case actually saw print. My editor thought it was too risky, even after the conviction." She took a sip of coffee and motioned for the waitress to bring some more.

"Your editor was right," Sam agreed.

Jennifer noted Belle's use of the words "back to." Sounded like she was an excellent match for the *Eye*. Why would she want to go back where integrity — and playing by the rules — was a necessity?

"DeSoto wrote me letters from prison." Belle smiled at the waitress who filled her cup and then shooed her away. She'd finished the burger and licked the ketchup off the side of her hand. Now she was on to the cheese fries. "I never answered any of them, and he seemed to lose interest after a few weeks. But about a month or so ago, the letters started back up again after Hovey filed the motion. Then the D.A. called me last week to let me know DeSoto was coming out."

"That's fast," Jennifer observed.

"Hovey worked in the fast lane," Belle assured her. "I figured my best bet was to let DeSoto think there was a man in my life, that I wasn't interested anymore, and that it wouldn't be just me if he came calling."

"But it was," Jennifer stated.

"Yep, but that's because they let him out even earlier than I thought they would. Hopefully he's got the message by now."

"You said you didn't expect Sam to see the announcement. Why would you expect DeSoto to see it?"

"I told my coworkers and my neighbors it was coming out. They all think it's legit. If he asks around for me, they'll mention it to him."

Great. Just in case anyone had missed it in the newspaper, Belle had made sure that all of Atlanta thought Sam and Belle were engaged.

"Is there any real reason to believe he'd be a threat to you?"

"I told you. Her apartment was trashed. And the man killed his wife. What more do you need?" Sam stated.

"Allegedly killed his wife," Jennifer reminded them. "I thought you said there was an actual threat."

"It was a cut-and-paste thingie put together from newspaper headlines," Belle explained. "It was mailed to my house."

"Why do you think it's from him?" Jennifer asked.

Belle shrugged. "Timing. And who else would it be from? Interviewing people about aliens landing in their barns and ghosts in their attics who do the laundry every Tuesday doesn't usually create an I-want-you-dead response."

"But you said he has no reason to be angry with you," Jennifer said.

"None except for not answering his letters from prison," Sam pointed out.

"And not waiting for him until he got out. Why don't you go back home to your family in North Carolina?" Jennifer suggested. That seemed like a perfect solution, at least to her.

"I certainly don't want him following me there. I can't take that risk."

The fake engagement might have worked, but only if the threat hadn't been serious. It wasn't something Jennifer would ever do, not even in a novel, but, hey, she wouldn't befriend some wife killer either. Or wolf down a burger like that. Or move in on somebody else's man. But the break-in had moved the action to a whole other field. "What if he doesn't buy the story?"

"DeSoto is not a maniac. I should be fine, once he calms down. He's a reasonable man, or at least he always was to me," Belle assured her.

"Right. A reasonable man who paid to have his wife murdered and sent you a death threat," Sam said.

Belle sighed. "*May* have sent. I wouldn't even be here if Sam hadn't insisted I come back with him. If DeSoto shows up again and threatens me, I'll change my identity and leave — at least until they nail that sucker in the retrial, which they'll do now that Hovey's not around to defend him. But I'm a journalist and that's a last resort. I want my byline to read Belle Renard."

Finally, something Jennifer could relate to. She'd never consider letting a publisher put out her books — assuming she ever sold one — under a name other than her own.

"When I found Belle —" Sam began.

"How did you find her?" Jennifer asked.

"Oh, Sam knows where I live," Belle offered.

"As I was saying," Sam rushed on before Jennifer could comment. He obviously didn't like the look in her eye. "When I found Belle, she told me DeSoto was already loose and she showed me what had happened to her apartment. I couldn't leave her in Atlanta."

"You should have moved," Jennifer said. "And gotten an unlisted phone number."

"Do you know how hard it is to find a decent apartment in Atlanta? I'm not going to let that jerk force me to give up where I live and certainly not my job, not until I've tried everything. Don't you see? If I move, all he has to do is follow me home one day."

Attractive, foolish, and stubborn — a deadly combination.

"Okay, but why choose Sam as your fiancé?" Jennifer asked.

"The last thing I remember Sam saying to me when we broke up was, 'If you ever need anything, I'll be there for you.' "

Broke up. Which meant there had been a relationship. She threw a none-too-friendly look at Sam.

"And when was that?" Jennifer demanded.

"Almost fifteen years ago," Sam said, meeting her eyes.

"But you meant it, didn't you?" Belle asked.

"It seems to me the operative phrase here is 'broke up,' " Jennifer interrupted, "as in the relationship was over, done, kaput. Haven't you met someone since Sam?"

"Lots of someones, but none like him."

Jennifer rolled her eyes. Sam may not get

it, but there was more going on here than some death threat. "And the photo?"

"Was taken at UNC's homecoming dance our sophomore year," Belle stated. "It was the only one I could find with me and some good-looking fellow in formal attire. We haven't changed so much since then, have we, Pepper?"

Oh, please. And Belle still knew exactly where she kept that photo, even after her move to Atlanta and however many in between.

"Okay. Now explain to me what you were doing in a bathrobe in Sam's apartment." Jennifer folded her arms and settled back against the padded bench. She'd never claimed any hold over Sam, but she wasn't about to let some woman snooker him away from her, especially not under these circumstances.

Jennifer reached over and smoothed Sam's hair down. He grabbed her hand and kissed her palm, but she jerked it back. His fault or not, she was not in a particularly affectionate mood, especially not with Belle sitting there staring at them.

"I got a call early Sunday morning," Sam said, "from one of the guys at the *Telegraph* asking what the heck was going on, why I hadn't told them about Belle, and if I needed a place to hide when you found out. I thought he was kidding until I opened the style section of the *Constitution.* I put in a call to a friend who works there. They don't normally give out information about who puts what in the paper, but as I was the prospective groom, he told me it was Belle. I drove up and found her. When she explained what was going on, I insisted she follow me back to Macon. At least if she's with me, I know she's safe."

Sam slipped an arm behind Jennifer.

"I hate to be a bore," she said, "but I still haven't heard an explanation for the bathrobe."

"Better the bathrobe than nothing at all." Belle winked at Sam and Jennifer came straight up in her seat. "Look, I only grabbed a few of my things. The place was a mess. I forgot pajamas."

That would be the first thing Jennifer would pack if she planned to be away overnight, especially in some strange man's apartment.

"So now you've moved in."

"It was late when we got back," Sam said. "I planned to settle Belle someplace safe today, but I've been busy tracking you down. I need to check out what's going on with DeSoto, see if I can find out exactly where he is. As a matter of fact, I was wondering if you might let Belle stay —"

Jennifer narrowed her eyes at him. Surely he didn't mean . . .

"That wouldn't work," Belle insisted. "You don't want to get Jennifer mixed up in all this, Sam. He's been talking about you nonstop since he picked me up. I know how crazy he is about you."

Jennifer sighed. What kind of answer could she give to that?

"You're right," Sam agreed. "We don't want to endanger anyone else."

"But won't DeSoto find Sam?"

"I doubt he'll look further than my apartment. This is a man who hired his dirty work done. And Sam's address isn't listed anywhere publicly. Surely DeSoto's legal defense dried up most of his money. I should be just fine here in Macon."

"So what are you planning to do while you're here?" Jennifer asked.

"I thought I could help Sam." She turned toward him. "I heard through the grapevine that you were coauthoring Hovey's autobiography."

Every fiber of Jennifer's being went on edge. It was one thing for Belle to move in on her man, but now she was trying to move in on her work with Sam, too.

"That can wait," Sam told her. "We need to get your situation settled first. I'll alert the authorities that you're —"

"No!" Belle shouted and then lowered her voice. "That wouldn't be a good idea. We shouldn't draw anyone's attention to us. This should all blow over in a few days, a couple of weeks at the most."

"A couple of weeks?" Jennifer said.

"Days. I meant days." Belle smiled that little-girl smile of hers.

Chapter 10

Thank goodness Belle was gone, tucked safely away at Sam's place. Out of sight, but certainly not out of mind. And Jennifer and Sam were alone, finally, for the first time all evening, with more to talk about than they could possibly have time for.

Jennifer grabbed a beer for him and a ginger ale for herself out of the fridge, and they sat on the floor, their backs propped up against her sofa, legs stretched out. They were miles away from where they'd been Saturday night, dancing in each other's arms. Now they were as awkward as two sixteen-year-olds on their first date with no idea of what to say to each other.

She stroked Muffy's fur. The dog lay between them, her head resting on her owner's knee. Jennifer felt as though she should talk to Sam about her feelings toward him, but she couldn't let go of her anger, even if it wasn't his fault. What could she say to him anyway? Heck! She didn't even know what to call him. Pepper?

The word made her seethe. Its very existence made her feel as though she didn't know him.

Even worse was how Belle was manipulating him. Something in her story didn't sound right. The police should have been able to subpoena DeSoto's phone records without any trouble, and Sam would know it, too, if he wasn't so busy protecting her. And what was all that about helping Sam with his book?

She had no idea how to bring up her doubts about Belle without sounding unreasonable and, heaven forbid, jealous. She opened her mouth to give it a try, but what came out was a safer subject.

"Suzie Turner was waiting for me when I got home yesterday afternoon. She was looking for you."

Sam stole a glance in her direction. "Who's Suzie Turner?"

"Suzanne Gray's niece. Sam, she doesn't think her aunt committed suicide."

He sighed heavily and took a healthy swallow of beer. "I knew we'd run into at least one."

"One what?"

"Doubter. A family member. A close friend. There's usually at least one who doesn't want to accept suicide."

"Suzie is a reasonable person. She and Suzanne were really close, and she didn't even tell her good-bye. And there's one more thing, Suzie says Suzanne was afraid of death."

"Most of us are. But most of us don't talk about death unless we're thinking about it. You're not helping your case."

"But you doubt that it was suicide yourself."

"We need more than instinct, Jennifer, and more than one relative saying it couldn't be so." He was chugging that beer.

"Okay, how about Suzanne's lack of a computer or a typewriter? Suzie says her aunt didn't own either."

"So she borrowed one. The library has them available for public use."

"She died the night of Hovey's funeral, Sam. If she put together that death scene all by herself, she had lots of preparations to make. I can't see her taking time to run to the library to compose and print up a suicide note when all she had to do was take up pen and paper."

"I got the coroner's report. I stopped by the police station in between visits to your place."

No doubt with Belle in tow.

"It's what we expected," he went on. "There was evidence of an unhealthy ingestion of sleeping pills. There was a lot of the drug in her blood. And she'd drunk a good deal of whiskey. It would have made for a lethal combination. But she died from exposure."

That made the whole idea of murder less probable. "Then there was no indication of homicide."

Sam shook his head.

"I want to see her clothes," Jennifer insisted, drawing her legs up under her and turning to face him.

"Why?"

"You said she had on white satin shoes, the dye-to-match kind, I'm sure. Ever walked in those things?"

Sam raised an eyebrow at her.

"I suppose not. They're treacherous unless they've been scuffed from walking over pavement. My dad used to run sandpaper over the soles before he'd let me go out to a formal dance. Only here's the hitch. You walk in them too much outside and you ruin them. The frost would have been slick as glass even if she'd scuffed the soles first. Even if she managed somehow not to fall, there'd be wet stains around the edges from walking through that grass, despite its being frozen. The pavement alone would have made the bottoms a mess. So what condition are those shoes in and was there a second pair found at the scene?"

"I don't know. I'm not sure how we could arrange for a look," he said.

"If the police don't keep them as evidence, and I don't see how they could if the coroner rules her death a suicide, they'll come back to her next of kin. That would be Marjorie Turner, Suzie's mom and the one who's so fond of you, right? And if you can't get her to let us see them, I'm sure Suzie will find a way."

"Okay," Sam agreed, "but there's another possible explanation for her death that you don't seem to have thought about."

"That someone helped Suzanne die? Oh, yes, I have. If this was suicide, Sam, I think she had help. And that's illegal."

"Exactly my point."

"You suspect it may have been the sister. No way. Kin only help if the person is terminally ill and suffering. Her sister would have had her in therapy or under observation in some hospital, especially considering how close she was to her niece. No, if Suzanne had help, it had to be someone who was as screwed up as she was. In other words, a best-friend type. Have you talked with the co-owner of her business, Kelli Byers? According to Suzie, she's the one with the computer."

"Not yet. She hasn't returned any of my phone calls. I did get a brochure, in care of the *Telegraph*, in the mail, so my guess is she plans to continue the business on her own."

"If she worked with Suzanne on a daily basis, she knows who her close friends were, who might have helped her kill herself, assuming Kelli didn't help her herself."

"So we've gone from murder to assisted suicide."

"Nope. I'm still holding out for murder," Jennifer said. "If Suzanne's coat and a second pair of shoes were left in her car, I'll grant you the thin possibility of suicide, but only if the satin shoes are messed up. No coat and no second pair of shoes, it's definitely assisted suicide or murder."

"On the basis of a coat and a pair of shoes?"

On the face of it, that did sound rather stupid. "It was really cold that night, cold enough to freeze to death. Suzanne needed the use of her fingers to set the scene, if she was the one who did it, and that would have taken a good bit of time. She obviously wanted everything perfect. Why get cold, fumble around, and mess things up? And why torture herself in the meantime? People commit suicide to end their suffering, not compound it. No, if she did it, she was dressed for the weather right up until the moment she took up those flowers and lay down to die."

"Not everybody wraps up in a blanket to eat ice cream like you do."

"I only do that in the winter."

"July Fourth weekend is not winter."

"It was particularly breezy that day. Don't try to get me off the subject. Suzanne would have been cold. I'm assuming she didn't have on long johns under that sleeveless dress."

"Not that I know of."

"Of course not. It would have ruined the whole effect. And if it was suicide, the person assisting would not have been trying to destroy evidence, only doing as she or he was instructed. Suzanne would have looked around, once everything was set, thrust the shoes and the coat into the hands of her accomplice and told her or him to take them back to her car."

"Or take them home," Sam suggested.

"Or take them home," Jennifer repeated.

"Darn. But grant me that the lack of a coat and other shoes means we're dealing with a second person on the scene. And she'd need a light source. A flashlight or a lantern. You didn't mention one found at the scene."

"There wasn't one that I know of."

"And when did she take the sleeping pills and drink the whiskey? Before she set everything up? Or after? They'd take some time to work their way into her system. Would she really lie there, exposed in the cold like that, if the drugs hadn't already begun to work?"

"You do realize you're ignoring one huge problem with your murder theory?"

She turned and looked him full in the face. "What?"

"The why. What motive would anyone have to kill Suzanne Gray?"

"Well, she . . ." Drat. He was right. She'd been so caught up in the how, she'd forgotten all about the why.

"The woman was found dead on Hovey's grave," Sam reminded her, "obviously linking the two deaths. I don't think either of us ever seriously considered the possibility of a 'hit.' But if someone was, say, jealous of their relationship, what was the gain in killing Suzanne with

Richard already dead?"

She had no answer for that one.

"According to Suzie, Suzanne held some kind of fascination for men. Maybe a woman —"

"Richard was dead. You seem to keep forgetting that fact."

Right.

"Go ahead and check into the coat and the shoes if you get a chance," Sam said, offering that much as a peace settlement. "Now do you think we could let Suzanne's death go, at least for one night?"

"Sure." Jennifer stood up and put her empty can on the dining table. Then she came back and perched on the sofa arm. "You want to talk about something else? I don't like Belle staying with you."

There it was, out in the open, but he'd asked for it.

"I'm not all that crazy about it either," Sam said, draining his beer and shifting uncomfortably. Obviously this change of topic was not the one he had in mind.

She paused, but he didn't offer anything else.

"When did you find out she'd moved to Atlanta?" she asked.

"I saw it mentioned in the alumni magazine."

So he watched for her name. Or maybe it simply caught his eye when he was checking his class notes.

Sam stroked the dog, starting at Muffy's ears and running down her back. He didn't once look up at Jennifer. Muffy stretched and sighed contentedly. At least she was getting something out of all of this.

"Why didn't you call her, ask her to lunch?" Jennifer asked. The moment she said it, she realized maybe he had. Belle said it had only been two years since she'd last spoken with Sam.

Two years. It must have been right around the time that Jennifer and Sam had met.

A strange expression settled across Sam's face. "You need to remember it was before I knew you. She called me. We got together a few times. She was trying to get established in the area as a journalist. I introduced her around. That's about all there was to it. My relationship with her is long over. Belle's no longer a part of my life."

Oh, yes, she was. She made sure of it when she printed that engagement announcement. And how much a part of his life had she been fifteen years ago?

"Why don't you like her?" he asked.

Jennifer slid off the sofa arm and back down onto the floor, facing him. "She's moving in on you."

Sam chuckled. "Don't be ridiculous. She's not moving in on . . . Don't tell me you're —"

Jennifer threw up her hands. "I misspoke. I meant moving in *with*." Men could be so clueless. "Let's not lose the thread here. Remember what you told me when we first met? The skill that makes you a good investigative reporter is being able to tell when someone is telling the truth. Something about Belle makes me uneasy." Hah! That was as understated as she'd ever manage. "And I certainly don't like the idea of her working with us while she's here."

"Why not? Belle could be a lot of help. She knew Hovey."

"What?"

"I introduced them. He was a good person to know because he was involved in so many high-profile cases. Most all the journalists knew him. And Belle's a competent reporter despite . . ."

"Despite what?"

"Despite where she works." He reached long and put his empty beer bottle on the floor, past the edge of the sofa. "I don't understand why you're so suspicious of her. Getting involved with Simon DeSoto, stupid as it may be, is exactly the sort of thing I know Belle would do. Besides, I saw the threat when I was at her apartment. It exists."

"How about DeSoto's letters?"

"She showed me three of the envelopes. They were postmarked from prison. She said she was too embarrassed to let me read the actual letters."

"So you think she really is in danger, that he's the one who was in her apartment."

He grabbed Jennifer's hand and pulled her over to him. Then he put his arm around her and drew her closer. Muffy yelped, then sighed, and allowed herself to be squashed between them. "I don't know, but I'm not willing to take the chance that she's not in danger. Belle asked for my help. I won't walk away from her."

"I don't want you to," she lied, snuggling closer and resting her head on his shoulder. What she so admired about Sam was exactly what had landed him in this mess. "But you know that old joke about the woman who picks up the snake and then is all surprised when it bites her. Do you know what you've just picked up?"

Sam pulled away and turned to look at her. She'd said too much. That's what she was afraid would happen. Honesty could get a person into a whole lot of trouble. Belle wasn't even there and yet Jennifer had played right into her hands.

"Belle is a complex woman," he said, "very competitive, but she's not evil. She simply goes after what she wants."

"I can relate to that," Jennifer said, wondering if Sam had any idea what it was that Belle wanted.

He shook his head. "No, you can't. You want to get published, and you'll do almost anything to see that happen. But you'd never hurt anyone in the process, not even someone as despicable as that literary agent Penney Richmond."

"That was all a big misunderstanding," Jennifer insisted, blushing. "Planning that murder was research for a book."

"Exactly my point. Everything you do, you do with so much passion. That's one of the things I love so much about you. But if achieving your dream meant hurting someone then you'd let it go."

Had Belle hurt Sam? Was that why they broke up?

"Tell me about it." She turned her face toward him, their noses almost touching.

"About what?"

"Meeting her in college, dating her." It was hard to imagine what Sam must have been like back then.

He pulled back. "I don't think going over past relationships is particularly healthy."

"I agree. But I need to know who we're dealing with because, Sam, in my gut I don't like any of this."

"She just needs a place to lie low. You're acting like she's dangerous."

Danger had all sorts of connotations. Not all of them had to do with physical harm.

Sam's beeper went off. He reached down, pulled it out of his pocket, and read off the number.

"What is it?" Jennifer asked.

Sam stood up. "It's Marjorie Turner's number."

"What's Suzanne Gray's sister doing calling you at this time of night?"

"I don't know. Mind if I use your phone?"

Jennifer scrambled to her feet. "Of course not. You know where it is." She wanted to listen in, but she had something she had to take care of. She ducked into the bedroom and was back just as Sam was hanging up the receiver. He reached for his coat.

Jennifer shoved a brown paper bag into his hands.

"What's this?"

"Pajamas and a robe for your houseguest. And a bottle of conditioner. What'd Marjorie want?"

"She doesn't know what to do about the body. The medical examiner has released it for burial. Suzanne's note specified that she wanted to be cremated, but Marjorie thinks she'd have preferred to be buried next to Richard."

"That could be a problem."

"Right. Richard's family is insisting that they'll never allow it."

Jennifer grabbed her own coat out of the closet, shrugged into it, dug her gloves out of the pockets, and pulled them on.

"Where do you think you're going?"

"With you."

"Wait just a minute. Marjorie lives on a dairy farm all the way out past the southeast part of town. Besides, she's made it clear that she won't speak to anyone but me."

"That means no other journalists, right?" Jennifer drew her scarf around her neck.

"Right."

"Well, then, she didn't mean me. And you've got to remember not to mention Suzie because her mother doesn't want her talking to you, or me, or, I suspect, anyone."

"Why?"

"I haven't got that one completely figured out yet, but she's probably overprotective. Maybe she's afraid Suzie's going to stir up some trouble."

"And she's probably right. If she'd found me yesterday, I'd have sent her straight home."

"She's not a child, Sam. She's twenty-one, even if she doesn't look it and is still living at home. Maybe Marjorie has a reason to keep things quiet. Everybody's got a past. Did you check into Suzanne's?"

He stole a quick kiss. "She doesn't have a criminal record, if that's what you mean. Now, I've got to go. It's been a long day and you need to get to bed." Then he touched the end of her nose with his index finger.

He should never have done that. It was far too condescending a gesture.

"Look, you can either let me ride in your car, or you can explain to Ms. Turner why some strange woman is following you around in a VW Bug, but I'm coming with you. Besides, you need me with you."

"And exactly why do I need you, other than all the obvious reasons?"

"Because, as I said before, I think like a woman. You don't know the right questions to ask."

"Oh, yeah? Like what?"

"Like who Suzanne was likely to have borrowed something from the day she died."

"Borrowed? Are you still talking about that —"

"Watch the adjectives," she warned.

"— that wedding theory?"

"Oh, you soooooo need me. I hate to admit this, but I think the tabloids got it right. Suzanne was dressed like a bride. Who else wears lace gloves these days? Something old: anything from underwear to cologne. Something new: most likely the dress. Something blue: the ribbon in her hair. The something borrowed and the person she borrowed it from — that may be of some help to us. She may have confided in her sister, even shown the item to her if she didn't get it from her."

"Makes sense, but at this point, I think the woman is more concerned about where she's going to lay her sister to rest."

"So what beef did Richard's family

have with Suzanne?"

"I don't know. All Marjorie said over the phone was that they didn't want her anywhere near him — not in life and certainly not in death."

Chapter 11

"I don't mind a person having friends, but just how many women do you have and do you have to bring them all with you?" Marjorie Turner asked, holding open the battered screen door to her kitchen and looking Jennifer up and down. She bore almost no resemblance to her sister or her daughter. She was tall and rawboned, and her face, without a trace of makeup, showed the effects of too much sun.

She pushed back a wisp of gray hair and said to Sam, "Your girlfriend's already here."

"What?" Sam began.

"What?" Jennifer echoed. She looked past Marjorie. Belle waved from one of the chrome chairs at the dinette set, a huge grin on her face. Then she was up and at the door, all over Sam, wrapping her arms around him, nuzzling his neck and whispering something in his ear. Jennifer caught ". . . play along. I didn't know what else to do."

Jennifer stood stunned, too appalled to do anything, while Marjorie loudly cleared her throat. Sam gently disentangled himself.

Out loud Belle said, "Mrs. Turner called our place first, sweetheart. I was afraid you might have turned off your pager while you were having your meeting with Miss Marsh, so I came right over."

Our place? Oh, she was so going down.

"She told me she wouldn't speak to anyone but you," Belle went on, "and I knew you wouldn't want to miss whatever she had to tell you."

"She said it was all right," Marjorie said. "I assumed that it would be since she answered your phone. Living together, huh? Young people these days! Not how I was brought up."

"Or me," Jennifer agreed. No one should have to live with Belle.

"And you are . . ."

Sam's face had a strange, deer-in-the-headlights look. Jennifer knew him well enough to know he wasn't about to play out a scene and lose Marjorie's confidence, but he obviously had no clue how to handle the situation. "Actually, she's —"

"Sam's secretary," Belle finished.

"I didn't think you journalists had secretaries," Marjorie said.

"They don't," Jennifer snapped.

"They like to be called administrative assistants these days," Belle explained.

"Well, whatever. You all get yourselves inside so I can close this door before every bit of heat flies out of this house. I've got a pot of coffee brewing. But you've got to keep your voices down. Vic's asleep. He's got to get up before dawn to take care of the livestock, and he doesn't want to be bothered by none of this anyhow. Says Suzanne's about as much trouble dead as she was alive."

The rhythmic purr of snoring drifted from the hallway.

"I usually stay up until our daughter gets home. They don't let her off at the Starvin' Marvin until after midnight. He hears the phone ringing and he gets all upset, thinking something's happened to our Suzie. He shot straight up out of the bed when the medical examiner's office called. Sounds like he managed to get on back to sleep. I swear, that man could sleep standing up, and keep half of Georgia awake sawing logs while he was doing it."

Marjorie pointed at the chairs at the dinette, and they each dutifully took a seat.

"Now I don't want anything I tell you in

the newspaper," Marjorie warned Sam, wiping her hands on her apron. "That's why I called you and not somebody else. I know I can trust you because you did such a fine job writing up what happened to poor Suzanne and keeping those gruesome photos out of the paper. Some of those other reporters twisted everybody's words around this away and that. They published all sorts of things that're nobody's business, trying to make her seem crazy. That tabloid in Atlanta even mentioned some trouble Suzanne got herself into in high school years ago."

Jennifer stole a glance at Belle. If she was insulted, she hid it well.

"Can you imagine?" Marjorie went on. "That Lewis Spikes boy. He fancied she liked him. Hah! He should have been so lucky. They had the nerve to print everything anybody would tell them, and then call here day and night expecting me to talk to them. Thank the good Lord they didn't make it to the cemetery until after the police had removed her body. Heaven only knows what kind of pictures they would have printed." She shook a finger at Sam. "I told them flat out on the phone that you're the only reporter I'll speak to. I wouldn't give you two cents for the lot of them. Vultures. I don't want no media circus, but I have to lay my baby sister to rest somewhere. Her dying like that." Marjorie shook her head. "It seems almost a sin not to let her lie next to that man for eternity."

Finally, the woman had come up for air.

"How well did you know Richard Hovey?" Jennifer asked.

"I didn't, except from seeing him on the TV every now and again." Marjorie got up, took two more mugs down from the cabinet, and poured four cups of coffee. "But Suzanne talked about him so much, I came to feel like I did. She told me he was the one she'd waited her whole life for. She'd never married, you know. She found him just in time, too."

"What do you mean?" Sam asked.

"Suzanne was thirty-nine." Marjorie handed around the mugs. "Now you watch it. That coffee's really hot. I use a percolator, not one of those drip thingamabobs. I told Suzanne it wasn't no use in having a man just to have him, but she was bound and determined to be married before she was forty. She only had four months to go."

"Her birthday's in June then," Jennifer said.

"June sixteenth."

"When I talked to you earlier, you mentioned that they met through her business," Sam stated.

"That's right. O Happy Day Delivery Service. She ran it out of her home. Balloons, candy, some flowers."

"Sounds like a pleasant way to make a living," Jennifer observed.

Marjorie nodded. "Not that it was much of a living, but she enjoyed it. It was like she borrowed other people's joy. I think that's why she did it. That and it gave her a chance to sing, as she put it, professionally. She never had the opportunity to go for it big time, but oh, my, what a voice that girl had. Sang every Sunday morning in the choir at church. Sweetest voice this side of heaven." She pulled a jug of milk out of the refrigerator, filled a small pitcher, and set it on the table with some spoons, next to the sugar bowl.

"Did Hovey use her service?" Sam asked, taking a sip of black coffee.

"Oh, lordy no. 'Bout six months ago his ex-wife hired her to take a bunch of balloons to his house. Wanted him back, she did. Suzanne usually has a couple of high school kids from down the way doing her deliveries or, if'n it's during the day, my

Suzie, except when her customers want someone to sing, which is what this was. Mrs. Hovey gave her a key and had her fill the entire downstairs of the house with balloons. She had to get some kind of expensive wine and go by Luigi's to pick up some sort of special appetizer that was Mr. Hovey's favorite. Then she was to wait until Richard came home, hand him a dozen red Mylars shaped like hearts and sing 'The Second Time Around,' but she opened her mouth and 'The Way You Look Tonight' came out instead. And that was it. They were both hooked. Fell in love right there in his living room."

"I bet that didn't go over well with his ex," Belle added, stirring her coffee. Jennifer noted she liked it black, too. One more thing she had in common with Sam.

Marjorie chuckled. "You know I don't believe it did. By the time Ruth showed up about five minutes later, right on cue, it was all over but the crying. But one can't deny true love. Which is why I called you. When I spoke with Richard's parents — they own the grave plots on either side of him — they said there was no way, excuse my language, in hell they'd let Suzanne be buried there. Can you believe it? Cussing at me like that right over the phone, and after I just lost my sister, too. Then they had that awful statement put in the paper today."

"What statement?" Sam asked. They'd all been so busy, not a one of them had even opened the day's newspaper.

Marjorie picked a clipping off the counter and tossed it to them. "I thought sure you would have seen this."

Jennifer read over Sam's shoulder. Belle was on his other side.

HOVEY FAMILY IN MOURNING, DENY ENGAGEMENT

Mr. Oliver Hovey, speaking for Mrs. Ruth Hovey and her family, denies the existence of a formal engagement between his son, Mr. Richard Hovey, and Miss Suzanne Gray, who was found dead on Mr. Hovey's grave last week. He insists that the publication of an engagement announcement in this paper was done in error. Miss Gray was described by the elder Mr. Hovey as an opportunist. According to the family, Mrs. Ruth Hovey and Mr. Richard Hovey were reconciling and had planned a wedding for late summer when Richard Hovey died unexpectedly.

Well, well. Seems someone was quite

mistaken, but whom?

"They have no right to slander the dead like that," Marjorie insisted, "now that Suzanne's not here to defend herself. I was wondering if I might have some legal rights, you know, to sue, to get them to print a retraction. And I want her buried right next to him, too. She was my baby sister, twelve years my junior. After Mom and Pop died, I practically raised her. I can't do nothing else for her. That's why I'd really like to do this."

"Why are his parents so belligerent?" Sam asked.

"My guess is they think it unseemly, her killing herself like that, on top of his grave, the earth not even settled over him. They're still claiming they'd never heard of Suzanne before they read your article in the newspaper, as if Richard was likely to tell them about her or any other woman he might be involved with. My bet is he knew how they'd react."

She leaned across the table toward Sam. "I really think it's that ex-wife of his. She's having a fit at the very thought of my Suzanne and Richard lying next to each other for all eternity. I think she's got her sights set on using one of those graves for herself. She stayed close with his folks. But I can tell you what I think is the fabrication: all that talk about her and Richard reconciling. She couldn't deal with the fact Richard had found his true love."

"That may be true but I doubt you have any recourse," Sam said. "An engagement has no legal standing under the law."

"I was afraid you'd say that." Marjorie stretched as though her back was giving her trouble. "I hope it wasn't too much of a bother me phoning you late like that. A person's supposed to honor the last wishes of the dead, but Suzanne never said one word to me about being cremated like was written in that note they found with her. And she said a whole lot to me about Richard. Guess I'll have to call the funeral home to go pick her up in the morning and then decide what to do."

"Did Suzanne tell you she and Richard actually planned to marry?" Jennifer asked.

"Of course. She talked about it all the time. I know she spoke to our minister about performing the ceremony, too, but I don't think they had a definite date picked out. I do know they were getting married no never mind what anybody says now."

"Did Suzanne have any close friends, someone else she might have shared her plans with?" Jennifer asked.

"You might talk to Kelli Byers, although I have to warn you she's an odd one. Suzanne and I weren't all that close. I mean she didn't tell me a whole lot, but I loved her. You've got to love family no matter what they do. It's just that we didn't have time to socialize much. Living on a farm requires that you be around. Animals don't understand it when you take a day off for lunch and a movie or go traipsing off to the mall, leaving them to fend for themselves."

"Do you know when she bought the dress she was wearing?" Jennifer added.

"I understand someone's gonna bring by her belongings sometime tomorrow. Until I see it, I won't know which one it was. When they asked me to come down and identify her, all they let me see was her face.

"I've got one more favor to ask of you," Marjorie told Sam, "seeing as how you're here and you've got these two women friends with you. I want to send a dress over for them to transport her in. It's not fitting for her not to have something to wear. Lord only knows what they wrap those bodies in. Only . . ."

Jennifer saw Sam steal a glance in her direction. She didn't say a word and, thank goodness, neither did Belle. If it was important to Marjorie to believe Suzanne's body would be clothed in more than a body bag, so be it.

"I don't think I can bear to go down to her house just yet, and I don't want Suzie down there either," Marjorie went on. "Do you think —"

"Absolutely," Belle jumped in. "Something simple and elegant."

"She's got a pale blue suit I plan to bury her in so don't take that, but there's a plain black dress I thought might be suitable —"

"Got a key?" Belle asked. Jennifer kicked her under the table, and Belle let out a loud "Ouch!"

"Was that your leg?" Jennifer asked. "So sorry."

"Where's her house?" Sam asked, ignoring them both.

" 'Bout a half mile up the road. Vic built her a little place on land we signed over to her." Marjorie rose and plucked a key from a glass dish on the counter. She handed it to Sam. Then she held the door open as they filed outside.

Belle shook her hand and slipped her a piece of paper with her name and Sam's phone number. "I'm really sorry about your sister. I know you've already got this number, but call if you need anything, or if you just want to talk."

Right. Belle would be right at the top of Jennifer's list if she ever needed sympathy.

Marjorie nodded and then hollered after Sam. "There's one more thing. I don't really expect to win this fight with the Hoveys. They're prominent people after all, they own the plot, they have a heck of a lot more money for lawyers' fees than I do, and as you said, I don't have any legal standing. Looks like I'll have to make a decision in the next couple of days. I can have Suzanne cremated, which is what she said she wanted done in that note she left, or I can have her buried next to Momma and Poppa, if'n I can't get the Hoveys to relent. I'm just wondering what you thought might be best. Vic don't have no opinion one way or the other."

Jennifer turned back. "Bury her. Before this is all over, I suspect the only thing Suzanne wouldn't forgive your doing is having her body cremated."

Chapter 12

The short trip down the road to Suzanne's offered no time for Jennifer to cool down. She got out of her little Beetle, slammed the door, and headed up the gravel driveway toward the front steps where Sam already stood. She had more than a few words for Belle and she wanted to say every one of them. Girlfriend, indeed! Our place, hah!

Belle got to the door first.

"What was all that nonsense you were telling Marjorie when we arrived?" Jennifer demanded at the front of the modest little house.

There were no outside lights on, no streetlights, and the house itself lay in complete darkness. Sam held his pocket flashlight under his arm while he inserted the key Marjorie had given him into the lock.

"Belle knew I was with you," Sam said. "You heard what she said. She was afraid I'd turned off my beeper and my phone, and she didn't want me to miss the information from Mrs. Turner."

And if he believed that . . .

"No way," Jennifer insisted, certain that Belle was fully capable of defending herself. "And what was that 'call me if you want to talk'?" She threw Belle a nasty look. Too bad she couldn't see it in the dark.

Sam pushed the door open. "Can we talk about this later?"

So Belle had managed it. Here she was fighting with Sam, or at least having an animated conversation, while Belle, quiet, probably for the first time in her life, looked on. Drat that woman. "Later will be perfect."

Sam fumbled along the inside wall for a light switch and then, suddenly, the room was bright.

Jennifer threw Belle another look, in case she'd missed the first one, and got back one of those innocent smiles. Then Belle pushed past her to go inside.

Suzanne's house seemed normal enough. Tiny, one story, built on a slab. It looked to be only three rooms, a fairly large living room/dining room/kitchen combo with two doors leading off, most likely to a bedroom and a bathroom. The structure itself was made of cinder blocks covered with plaster.

Simple, unpretentious, undoubtedly cold in the winter, not that Macon usually got all that cold.

The decor was drab and haphazard at best, but the place was fairly neat, except for a couple of dirty dishes in the sink, which was under a large window facing the street, and a drinking glass left on the counter. Surely Suzanne would have cleaned them and put them away before committing suicide. It was like wearing clean underwear while driving. If she knew she was going to die, wouldn't she want people to think she kept a nice house? Or was Jennifer the only one who would think of something like that?

The main room held nothing particularly out of the ordinary save for a vase of wilted roses, with a large red bow, placed prominently on the maple coffee table. The water had turned slime green. A sad reminder of what might have been.

The room was furnished with a simple, inexpensive, brown plaid sofa and chair, end tables with ceramic lamps that needed new shades, an area rug on the tile floor, and a really old TV set. Jennifer suspected there was a satellite dish in the yard out back. The only photo on any of the walls was one of Suzie Turner wearing a high school cap and gown.

Drab, however, ended at the bedroom door.

"Would you look at this?" Belle called from the doorway. "She saved the color for in here."

Jennifer and Sam followed her into the twelve-foot-square room.

The double bed was spread with a purple satin coverlet with half a dozen matching throw pillows hiding most of the headboard. A white stuffed cat perched on the center pillow, and a pile of bridal magazines sat next to the bed. The walls were painted lavender, and the single window had artificial purple and pink flowers draped across a gauzy white swag.

But even more striking than the girliness of the room was the sheer volume of paper stacked about. The entire top of Suzanne's small desk was covered with what looked like brochures, and the oak dresser was mounded with swatches of fabric. A single poster of a beach at sunset proclaiming Barbados to be the most romantic honeymoon destination stretched above the desk. And next to it hung a candid photo of Richard Hovey, enlarged to an eight-by-ten and framed.

"Admit it," Jennifer demanded.

"You were right," Sam conceded. "The woman was obsessed with getting married."

"Not obsessed," Belle corrected. "You obviously have no idea how much effort goes into planning a wedding."

"Oh, and I suppose you do," Jennifer said.

Belle gave her a long look. "Maid of honor twice. I'd say I have some experience."

Unfortunately not as the bride.

"But it's not for me," Belle went on. "I say keep things simple. I don't believe in long engagements. Justice of the peace, a little motel somewhere, a lock on the door, and lots and lots of room service, at least a week's worth. You like things simple, don't you, Sam?"

She could kill her here and now. Sam would be the only witness. Would he really testify against her?

Sam, wise man that he was, didn't utter a sound.

Focus, she ordered herself and, without a word, picked up a cluster of swatches, all samples of lace, from the piles on top of the dresser. She touched another bunch of satins and a third of silks ranging from eggshell to bright white in varying weights and quality. A fourth stack in the burgundy-to-pink families had to be for the maid of honor and bridesmaids' dresses. She noted the cardboard tag attached to each group: La Boutique Nuptiale.

"All of this planning for only twenty minutes?" Jennifer uttered, more to herself than out loud.

"That's just the core part of the ceremony," Belle assured her. "With a good vocalist and written vows you can stretch it another thirty minutes. But weddings are really weekend-long affairs these days, what with the dinners and the reception. And none of that includes the showers and the bachelor and bachelorette parties."

"What's all that cost?" Jennifer asked.

"Thousands of dollars," Belle assured her. "But what the heck, you only do it once."

Not according to the Census Bureau.

Sam stood shaking his head, in seeming shock. He was flipping through stationery samples on the desk. "Invitations. Brochures from florists. She's got everything here from romantic getaways in Savannah to world cruises." Jennifer joined him. She noted a business card: Talley's Travels.

"Hey, would you look at this," Belle offered. "She's even got pamphlets on china patterns."

"I wonder if she was actually registered anywhere," Jennifer said.

"So do you believe it now?" Sam asked. "She puts all this effort into her dream wedding and then the groom dies on her. You can't still think her death was —"

Jennifer stomped his foot, and Sam let out a loud yelp. He knew better. Not in front of Belle.

"Think it was what?" Belle asked, suddenly all ears.

"Think it was unrequited love," Jennifer said. "You heard what Marjorie said about the Hoveys' attitude. Suzanne may not have been what they had in mind for a daughter-in-law, but after looking at all this, I don't think anyone could deny the relationship. Shouldn't we at least look in her closet? That is what Marjorie sent us here to do."

Belle slid back the bifold door to a closet crammed full of clothes, which Belle immediately began pawing through. "I see things in here that date back at least to the eighties. Lots of lime green and orange. And, guess what, purple. And red. This woman must have never thrown away a thing."

"Just look for the black dress," Jennifer reminded her. "Do you think we should take anything else?"

"Like what?" Belle asked. "I think it's a remote chance in hell anyone will dress her. Do you really think they'd try to put pantyhose on a corpse?"

Before Jennifer could answer, the blare of police sirens filled the house, blue lights flashing through the windows.

"What the . . ." Sam began.

They abandoned the bedroom for the living room. Belle started toward the front door, but Sam yelled at her to stay put as pounding started.

"Open up. Sheriff's department."

"Yes, sir." Sam motioned Jennifer and Belle up against the wall, out of direct line of the door, and then cautiously opened it.

Three deputies, their weapons drawn, entered. Both Belle and Jennifer's hands shot up. The first deputy looked about the room and then holstered his gun. "It's all right," he called to the men behind him and then spoke something Jennifer couldn't catch into a walkie-talkie. "Sam, what the heck are you doing here?" he asked.

"We're here at the invitation of Marjorie Turner, Suzanne Gray's sister." He offered the key Marjorie had given him.

"We'll have to check with Mrs. Turner. Sorry, but it's procedure. Wait here just a moment." He left the other two deputies inside. No one said a word. Heck, they didn't even breathe until he returned. "Okay. Mrs. Turner confirmed she authorized you being here. We had a report of suspicious activity —"

"Arrest them," a woman demanded, dressed in light blue stretch jeans and a shiny white plastic coat. Framed in the doorway, her chin high, bleached hair short and spiked, eyes circled black with liner, pink lipstick pale and shiny, and cheeks round and rosy with indignation, she looked like some strange comic-book version of an avenging angel. "Arrest them before they destroy the evidence."

Chapter 13

"Evidence of what?" Jennifer demanded. "Who *are* you?"

"That is none of your business, missy. Book 'em, Hank." The woman put both hands on her slender hips and glared.

One of the deputies leaned close to Jennifer's ear. "Her name is Kelli Byers. She's a looney tune. Lives just across the road. She's the one who reported the break-in."

"Excuse me?" the woman demanded. She looked young, probably in her early thirties, and she would have been striking in the soft light of a bar. Under normal light, which flashed off the studs and hoops circling one ear and most of the other, she looked more like a painted doll.

And so very out of place.

"Do you feel it necessary to converse with the enemy, Hank? My best friend on this earth, Suzanne Louise Gray, was driven to suicide by the likes of them." She pointed an accusatory finger. "And you officers of the law are doing nothing whatsoever to investigate." The finger — still accusatory — swung in Hank's direction. "Instead you let these Hovey hirelings come in here and destroy every trace of the greatest love this world has probably ever known." She let out a loud sob, but Jennifer noted there were no tears to go with it.

"Okay, we're done here." The first deputy held the door for the other two. "Just make sure you lock the place up good before you go," he told Sam and turned toward the door.

Kelli stepped in front of him. "Do something, Hank."

"Take it home, Kelli," he suggested, going around her and out the door. But the woman seemed firmly planted in place, her arms now crossed and her fingers tapping nervously against her sleeve. Her gaze darted back and forth from Sam to Jennifer to Belle, seemingly assessing the three-to-one odds.

"Let me guess. You're the maid of honor," Belle suggested.

"Would have been. In incandescent mauve shantung."

Nothing cut too low. Jennifer suspected a tattoo lurked here or there.

"You were Suzanne's business partner," Jennifer added.

"That's right. Bookkeeper, scheduler, product controller, investor. Suzanne was the talent. Now get out of here!"

She threw her hands up into something like a karate pose and hissed. The woman actually hissed. If she'd had a cross on her, Jennifer was convinced she would have pulled it out.

Sam, to his credit, smiled and offered her his hand. "Sam Culpepper, *Macon Telegraph.* Marjorie asked us to come by and pick up some garments for Suzanne's body when it's transported from the medical examiner's office."

"Oh." Kelli's cheeks grew an even brighter red. "She could have called me." She shook Sam's hand, making sure he couldn't miss her perfectly sculpted fake pink fingernails.

"We don't even know the Hoveys," Jennifer assured her. "We're really sorry for your loss."

"So you were friends with Suzanne," Belle said. "Did she tell you she planned to kill herself?"

Kelli glared. "Do you think I would have let her out of my sight if I'd known what she was going to do? Who will make the singing deliveries now? Her dying pretty much put me out of business, not that there was all that much business to begin with. Just what am I supposed to do with four hundred balloons and enough helium to float the coliseum?"

"Suzanne confided in you," Jennifer suggested. Kelli looked back and forth between Jennifer and Belle. It reminded her of the new girl at school being wooed by rival factions, only Jennifer suspected Kelli Byers wasn't used to being wooed by anybody. She looked like a loner.

"Only about the wedding. She met that man just months ago, and her life changed. Every breath she took was for Richard. I could hardly get her to the bowling alley anymore, and we had a standing date every Thursday."

And with those nails, too.

"It was off to this store and off to that one," Kelli continued. "She was way too busy. She kept saying Richard had standing in the community that he had to uphold. He had important acquaintances that all had to be invited. Their wedding was going to be the biggest social event that Macon has seen this millennium."

Of course this next thousand years was young yet.

Kelli took a soft pack of cigarettes from her coat pocket and shook one out. She lit it with an orange Bic lighter, drew in a great lungful of air, and then half-heartedly offered the pack around.

"She was crushed when Richard died, of course," Kelli said, "but she never said nothin' to me about killin' herself." Smoke escaped from her mouth in a great puff. "If she had, I would have stopped her. Men come and they go — boy, do they go — but I've not met a man yet worth dyin' over, especially not that one."

Jennifer and Sam exchanged glances. "Why not that one?" Sam asked.

"Let's just say it wasn't all heaven in paradise."

"Who was he seeing?" Belle, ever tactful, asked.

"My mama taught me never to speak ill of the dead. Your mama teach you anything?"

Kelli took another big draw on her cigarette and then shot Belle a spew of smoke. Score one for Jennifer's side.

"Don't take the black dress," Kelli said. "For her to wear. That's the one Marjorie told you to get, wasn't it? She bought it for her and Suzanne never once wore it. It hung on her like a sack and Suzanne detested black."

Kelli disappeared into the bedroom. They all followed, watching as she held her cigarette tightly between her lips and snatched a red polyester with a halter neck from the closet.

Jennifer couldn't help but feel sorry for Kelli as she accepted the dress. "Did you like Richard?"

"Never met the man. I always suspected Suzanne was a little afraid to bring him around me." She pulled open her coat and looked squarely at Sam. Smart man that he was, he looked away.

Kelli was most likely right about Suzanne wanting to keep Kelli away from Richard, but Jennifer suspected not for the reasons Kelli thought.

"You mentioned the possibility of another woman," Sam reminded her. "Was it his ex-wife?"

Kelli gave Sam a good once-over and smiled. "You want to come on over to my place?" She sidled up next to him. "We could have us a private conversation."

"Maybe some other time."

Maybe some other lifetime.

Kelli dropped the act, slumped back against the door, and lit another cigarette off the end of the first one. Then she lifted her foot, stubbed out the old one on the bottom of her high-heeled shoe, and dropped the butt to the floor. "Wasn't me that said anything about another woman. That was you." She pointed at Belle. "What I said was that he wasn't treatin' her right. He didn't take her out like he should. Didn't come 'round like he should either."

Ah, yes. Kelli had demonstrated what a good view she had of Suzanne's house.

Belle let her gaze sweep the room. "Maybe they preferred to meet elsewhere."

"What are you implyin'?" Kelli demanded. "You think what we have ain't good enough for a Hovey? Just where do you think Mr. Big-Time Lawyer came from in the first place? You damned smart-ass professional women. The hell with you!"

And with that, Kelli Byers left, slamming the front door behind her.

Chapter 14

Kelli's righteous indignation was still ringing in Jennifer's ears as she unlocked the door to her own apartment. Muffy practically knocked both Sam and her down, whining and yelping, complaining that she'd been left after dark by herself with no lights on. The biggest no-no in any dog's book.

She hugged Muffy's neck, and then fell, exhausted, into Sam's arms. It was late. How late, she didn't even want to know.

"We need to talk," he said.

"I know, but not tonight." They both knew better. They were too on edge, and she didn't want to say anything wrong. "You need to get home. You've got a houseguest."

He kissed her. "I'll call you tomorrow."

"I've heard that one before."

"I promise. Of course that's assuming I can get through to you," he added.

"What do you mean?" she asked.

"Your answering machine. Didn't you notice? It's blinking. Looks like you have a slew of messages and only about four of them are mine."

She stared at the flashing light and the little number. Normally it was the first thing she noticed when she opened the door to her apartment. But then she'd been a bit preoccupied when they'd been there earlier, and she hadn't thought once to look.

He kissed her once more, a sweet, yet passionate kiss that held more promise than they had strength to see through. She wished it was Saturday night all over again, that she'd let him say whatever it was he'd wanted to say, that she had never mentioned Suzanne Gray's name.

Then he pulled back. If he was leaving, he'd better do it now.

"Let's skip the call and make it lunch tomorrow," he suggested, touching her cheek. "Say about noon."

She nodded. "I'll meet you at the Bookshop Café around the corner from your office."

She shut the door after him, barred it, and went directly to the answering machine, hitting the button. The first four messages were indeed Sam's from earlier that day, wanting to know where she was and becoming a little more frantic with each beep. He did grovel nicely. She felt ashamed that she'd ever doubted him.

Beeeeep!

You're not home. Good! You and Sam must be off somewhere making up. Or maybe you're home and making up and I'm interrupting. Sorry. In that case, just ignore little ole me. Leigh Ann's voice fell to a whisper. *I told you he was crazy about you, Jen. Call me. I want details. By the way, I think I should warn you. After you left, Monique went into crisis mode. She's called an emergency meeting for tomorrow night. She adores Sam and she's determined to make you come to your senses. Please show up, Jen. There'll be hell to pay if you don't.*

Beeeeep!

My house. Tomorrow night. Seven sharp. Monique really missed her calling. She would have made a great drill sergeant. *I expect you here for a strategy meeting, and don't pretend you don't need our help because you do. Oh, yes, and I expect you to have pages from your novel to read next week. No excuses. It's been three weeks since we've heard a word you've written.*

Beeeeep!

Hey, girlfriend, it's Teri. Make that man crawl. Remember we have a contingency plan, just in case. You know I love Sam, but some things are unforgivable. And that Belle woman . . . oooweeee. You've got to get her out of the picture now because if you don't, you're going to be one sorry lady. I know I'm going to regret saying this, but I'm here if you need my help in any way. I mean it. Just call. Day or night.

Beeeeep!

Sweetie, I hope you haven't done anything rash. Sam's such a good guy. He'll make a wonderful father. Don't throw him away, at least not until we've had time to talk. In the background she could hear little Jonathan calling *Mommy, Mommy, I can't sleep,* and April saying *Go find your daddy, sweetheart. I'm on the phone. Sorry about that, Jen. It gets harder to find the good ones after you've turned thirty, you know. If you start over with some other guy, it'll put you at least two years behind and you'll be pushing into your mid-thirties before you can even consider having children. Love you.*

That April was always concerned about the gene pool and Jennifer's deteriorating egg supply.

Beeeeep!

Jen, it's Dee Dee. We've got a catering job scheduled for this Friday night. Don't forget. I'm counting on you to serve. Hope you're all right. I haven't heard from you in days.

Darn! She had forgotten.

Beeeeep!

Hey, pretty lady. Atlanta Eye's boy wonder, Teague McAfee. She should have known he'd show up. *How's your love life? I understand it's taken a direct hit. Ouch! Right in the heart. Told you that boyfriend of yours was not the man for you. So now you're available. I'm available.* Big surprise. *Give me a call, Marsh.* Sure, when hell freezes over. *I know Belle. I've worked with her. You'll call. Ciao.*

She sighed. Sometimes — no, all the time — she hated that man.

Beeeeep!

Miss Marsh, I mean, Jennifer, it's Suzie Turner. I'm calling you from work. I remembered something. You asked about how Mr. Hovey treated my aunt, like you wanted an example of how good he was to her. After she met Mr. Hovey, every Friday she received seven long-stemmed red roses, one for each day of the week. So that's where the roses at Suzanne's had come from. *I thought it was so sweet. Anyway, just thought you should know.*

Beeeeep!

I've got the first report back on Isabelle Renard. It was Mrs. Walker's voice. *I think you'll be most interested in hearing what I've found out. Call me immediately, my dear, whatever the time. I hope I need not remind you again that this is more important than whatever is currently occupying your time. The game is afoot.*

"Men are weak, dear. Surely you know that," Mrs. Walker assured her over the telephone.

"Men are not weak, at least not any more weak than women are," Jennifer insisted, digging a treat out of a bag on top of the refrigerator. Now that Muffy had her alone, she was convinced it was playtime. And why not? While Jennifer had been out running around all day and half the night, she'd been sleeping. One in the afternoon, one in the morning, it was all the same to her.

"Of course, you're right. We're all weak. That only compounds the problem, doesn't it? As I was saying, you can't let that woman stay under his roof. She'll have her way with him. She's ruthless to the core and, if what you've told me about her and DeSoto is true, she's a self-confessed seductress."

"Exactly what do you suggest I do? Sam won't turn her out, and I don't intend to take her in."

"Do you not have hotels in that town of

yours? Tell him to move her to one."

"Believe me, I'm working on it. What have you found out?"

"Well, Isabelle graduated from UNC the same year as your Samuel. She was no more than an average student, but not because she lacked intelligence. Her SAT scores were outstanding. She's high energy, very aggressive. She landed a job at a newspaper in Raleigh because she simply refused to leave the office after she was told they had no openings. She even slept overnight in their waiting area and then wrote up a feature article about her experience and turned it in the following morning. She likened the newsroom to a hospital emergency room, very flattering to the paper involved. And with her demonstrated tenacity, the editor felt she'd make a good reporter. She worked there for two years and then moved to Charlotte, where she was employed for another three years by a paper with a larger circulation. From there she went on to an even bigger newspaper in Philadelphia. More pay, definitely more notoriety. She had her eye on the *Washington Post* next I'm told, but then there was a most unfortunate incident."

"You don't say?"

"Oh, I do say. Isabelle wrote an article that garnered a good deal of national attention. It was about an elderly woman who set up a house of prostitution with her bridge-club friends so they could make enough money to pay for their prescription medicines."

"You're not serious," Jennifer interrupted.

There was a lengthy pause on the other end of the line. "Sex doesn't exist only among the young, my dear. Is that what you think?"

"No, I . . . I just meant . . ."

"That's quite all right. Apology accepted. There were rumors of a possible Pulitzer nomination. It looked as though she would have her pick of newspapers to work for."

"What happened?"

"That article she wrote . . . It seems it was a suspected work of fiction."

"Really?"

"Oh, I'm afraid so, dear. She crossed the ethics line. She had no sources whatsoever for her depiction, only a bunch of little old ladies who denied everything. Her editor bounced her fanny right out on the sidewalk. Didn't even give her the option of resigning."

"Oh, my." That was quite an image that formed in Jennifer's mind. Belle sprawled on a sidewalk. She rather liked it. "Did she ever admit any wrongdoing?"

"Goodness, no. She's still insisting her sources recanted because they were too embarrassed to have their little enterprise examined publicly. When the police investigated, they found nothing. Either the operation never existed, or once the article saw print, it was closed down and all evidence of it erased. So you can see that she stops at nothing to get what she wants. And I'm most afraid that what she wants is your Samuel."

Jennifer opened her mouth to protest, and then stopped. "What should I do?"

"Easier to tell you what not to do. Don't try to convince Sam of her danger. You'll only come across as a shrew, which will give her more of an advantage than she already has. The only way to win him —"

"I'm not sure I'm ready to win anybody."

"Of course you are, dear. If you're not, you'd best be prepared to lose him."

Lose Sam? She'd had one night and two days of feeling as though she'd lost him, and she didn't like it one bit.

"There's a reason, dear, that a young,

vigorous — I'm assuming that he is vigorous."

Jennifer blushed even though Mrs. Walker couldn't see her.

"I'll take your silence as acquiescence," Mrs. Walker continued. "There's a reason a vigorous male such as your Sam Culpepper isn't and has never been married. Did it occur to you that reason might be Isabelle Renard?"

No, it hadn't.

"Are you still there, dear? She could be the one, you know. The one from the past, the one who's prevented him from moving forward, at least until he met you. One mustn't toy with this idea of a past. It creates strong emotional ties. You're not working on a level field when two of the parties have a history, regardless of what that history may be. Are you understanding anything I'm saying to you?"

Jennifer cleared her throat. "I'm hearing you. I don't suppose your investigator turned up anything about Belle's involvement in the Simon DeSoto case?"

"No, but that doesn't surprise me if, as you've said, the police were keeping it quiet."

"She implied that she cohabited with DeSoto, or at least had access to his home.

There must have been neighbors, friends of DeSoto, someone who saw her at his place."

"I'll get my agent right on it. And you know what you must do."

"Okay, I'll see if I can get Belle to a motel."

"Tonight, my dear."

No way could she march back over to Sam's apartment at that point. "As soon as possible."

"Tonight, my dear." Mrs. Walker hung up, and the phone buzzed in Jennifer's ear.

Belle had won this round. She'd stay in Sam's apartment one more night. Jennifer could only hope that wouldn't be one night too long.

Chapter 15

"See anything yet?" Teri demanded, stomping her feet loudly and shivering so much that Jennifer couldn't possibly miss it. Earmuffs and double-layered mittens were not enough to keep out the cold.

"Not yet, but she'll be here," Jennifer assured her. She peeked past the crypt. The moon offered just enough light so that no one could approach Richard Hovey's grave undetected.

"So you think Hovey's wife is the one who's leaving the roses."

"Ex-wife, Ruth Hovey. She wanted him back, that much we know. And at this point, we don't have any other women in the equation."

"That man was hot," Teri offered.

"And scruple-free," Jennifer pointed out.

"Girl, put that bad boy in a suit, make him controversial, and throw in a million or two in his bank account, and no telling how many women he had after him."

"The only one I'm interested in at the

moment is the one buying the flowers."

Teri rubbed her hands together again. "I can't believe I let you drag me out of bed before daylight."

"At least you got more than three hours of sleep last night. Besides, you said you wanted to help. I think your exact words were 'if you need my help in any way, day or night' . . ."

"I think that was *call* me day or night. The part of my offer concerning my actual body only applied to daylight hours. Do you know when I last saw the sunrise?"

"Easter morning?"

"Seven years ago when my grandmother dragged me to services. Once a year is way too often, especially for something that happens every day." Teri shifted back and forth on the balls of her feet. "It's too cold for this. Why do you think I live in Georgia? It's supposed to be warm here."

"You were born here," Jennifer reminded her.

"That, too. A fortunate coincidence. But I still don't see why we had to trek all the way over here from the gas station. Why couldn't we just park on the road like everybody else?"

"We don't want her to see our car and

get scared away. Look, I told you I'd buy you breakfast. I didn't ask you to come, you know."

"Right. You just called me at midnight to 'inform' me you were going. What kind of person leaves her nutty friend to go alone lurking in some graveyard where bodies turn up? This woman had better hurry up and make her appearance. I do have a job to go to and I'm going to have hat hair all day." Teri tugged on her knit cap.

"She'll be here. She hasn't missed a morning yet. Which means she must have seen Suzanne Gray's body before the groundskeeper found it."

"That's assuming she didn't have something to do with putting her there," Teri pointed out, "if your assisted suicide or murder theory is true."

"Exactly," Jennifer agreed.

"Why are you doing this?"

Jennifer stole a sideways glance, but it was too dark to read Teri's features. She didn't like where that question might lead. "To find out who's putting the roses on Hovey's grave."

"That's not what I mean. Why are you trying to find out what happened to Suzanne Gray?"

"Because I don't believe she committed

suicide. And because her niece doesn't either."

"Yeah, but there's more to it than that, and, if you don't admit it, you're not being honest with me or yourself. Knowing you, it's probably both. You don't go chasing after suspects."

"I never said this woman was a suspect."

"Let me finish. You're a writer, not an investigator. If your involvement in this case has to do with proving to Sam —"

"I'm not proving anything to anybody," Jennifer snapped.

"Damn it, child. You are so out of touch with your feelings, you don't even know why you got yourself out of bed at six in the morning. Belle has moved in with Sam. According to you, she's even stated she intends to 'help' him with his work while she's living there. If you want him to know how essential you are to his life, you don't have to do it this way. Sam loves you because he does. Because you're a woman and he's a man. Because you're who you are, which — except for moments of insanity like this one — is a pretty terrific person."

"Thanks for the testimonial."

"Would you please just be quiet for two minutes? You don't have to show him you're some superduper —"

Jennifer slapped a hand warmer into Teri's hand.

"What am I supposed to do with this?"

"Whatever you want. Just be quiet." Teri didn't understand. She couldn't. This had nothing to do with Jennifer and Sam. Murder or suicide, Suzanne Gray loved her man — died for her man — and nobody cared, nobody except for a young woman who worked in a convenience store and adored her. Worse than that, the Hoveys were bent on belittling what happened to Suzanne. It wasn't fair.

"Crush the bag and hold it," Jennifer directed. "It gives off heat."

"It's not more than four inches square. I have a whole body here that's clamoring for some warmth. Just where am I supposed to put it? My toes are just a fond memory."

Remind Teri of a little physical discomfort, and everything else flew right out of her mind.

Teri stuffed the warmer inside her mitten, against her palm and let out a sigh. "You know Monique is not going to be pleased that we didn't wait for the meeting tonight before staking out the graveyard."

"Yeah, well, she'll just have to deal."

Teri shook her head. "You are either getting more independent with each breath you take or you're just plumb crazy. By the way, April brought an uncorrected proof of *The Case of the Missing Nuts* to group Monday night. She showed it to us after you and Sam left."

Jennifer blinked hard, staring straight ahead. "A book? A solid, not-on-eight-and-a-half-by-eleven-paper book?" It was hard to imagine.

"Yep. It will hit the shelves of the children's section in less than two months.

"It has a terrific cover with the title in huge letters and just below it April's name," Teri went on. "It's done in autumn colors. Barney, the flying squirrel, is depicted in full flight, the membranes between his little paws stretched tight. Personally, I thought he looked like a kite, especially with young Billy standing down below him. Just add a string —"

Jennifer shot her a sideways glance.

"No, really, it's great. Squirrels just aren't my thing. Billy's all round and cute. He's under a huge oak tree with piles of acorns and leaves everywhere."

"I wish I'd seen it."

"You will. She gave us each a copy. All of our names are in the acknowledgments. And you know the really weird part? When you read it bound like that, all professional, it's ten times better than it was when she was reading it to us in group. Somebody might actually go into a store and say, 'Wow, this looks like a great book for my kid.' "

"That's the whole idea."

"Right, but —"

Jennifer shushed her. She was certain she'd heard something, like the crunch of rubber on gravel. The pink glow from the sun suddenly burst outward, lightening the whole area. A bright blue compact hatchback stopped on the road just above the grave, and Jennifer laid a death grip on Teri's arm. The driver's side door opened and a figure emerged wearing a waist-length, light-colored coat that caught the light. Something was wrapped tightly around the person's head. Quickly the figure was at the grave, kneeling.

"C'mon." Jennifer pulled Teri forward.

"We could just get the license plate, you know," Teri suggested. "You don't think she's armed, do you?"

"Why would she be? Everybody here is already dead."

They circled around and came up behind the woman, careful to make as little noise as possible. They could hear her mumbling between sobs.

Jennifer touched her shoulder, and the woman promptly let out a bloodcurdling scream. Teri screamed, too.

The woman turned and clutched her chest. "You scared me half to death."

"I'm sorry, really sorry," Jennifer apologized, backing up. "We heard you crying and I thought maybe we could help."

The sun was up enough now that Jennifer could see the woman's tear-stained face, her eyeliner running. She clutched a single, long-stemmed red rose in her gloved hand.

"Kelli? Kelli Byers? Suzanne's maid of honor? *You're* the one who's been leaving the roses?" Jennifer asked.

"What the hell are *you* doing here?" Kelli demanded. Quickly, she wiped her face. She placed the rose on the grave, said something under her breath, and scrambled to her feet.

"You and Richard Hovey . . ." Jennifer began, for once at a loss for words.

"No." Kelli stamped her feet. "What do you mean? That's sick!"

"Hey, lady, you're the one leaving the roses on the man's grave," Teri pointed out.

"This is where Suzanne died," Kelli explained. "She doesn't have a grave for me to mourn at yet. Look, I've got to go." She turned and headed back toward her car.

"I'm sorry we scared you," Jennifer called after her. As soon as Kelli was in her car, Teri turned to Jennifer and said, "So that was the woman who called the police on you at Suzanne's? She's a piece of work."

"The very one. So what do you think?"

"I think Richard Hovey was doin' his fiancée's maid of honor."

Chapter 16

"You called Ruth Hovey from a pay phone and you asked her what?" Teri demanded. "Can't I even let you go to the bathroom by yourself without getting into trouble?"

Jennifer pulled her little car out of the parking lot of the Bob Evans Restaurant. They had been fed — pancakes for Jennifer and sausage gravy over biscuits for Teri — and pumped full of coffee.

"I asked her if she knows who Richard Hovey was waiting for the night he died," Jennifer repeated, heading east.

"I bet that ticked her off. What did she say?"

"I didn't mean to upset her. She said she wants to meet with me right away. Then she hung up."

"Do you suppose she knows about the rose petals?"

"Of course she knows. She probably had to arrange to have the house cleaned after his death. I'm sure his children are his heirs."

"And that one little question was enough to get her to agree to see you?"

Jennifer braked at a stop sign and shot Teri a sidelong glance. Then she turned left and headed out of town. "If she doesn't know the answer, I'm sure she's curious as hell."

"And thinks you do know. But you don't. You only suspect it was Suzanne. But what if it was Kelli? Or some other woman? What if it was her? What are you going to say when she asks you?"

"What I always do?"

"Right. You're going to wing it. And get yourself into even more trouble."

Teri pointed at a sign reading HOVEY'S HERMITAGE, and Jennifer headed the little car up the long driveway.

"Hermitage does not have a friendly connotation," Teri pointed out.

"Right, but we're here at Ruth's invitation, remember?" She parked on the side of the huge white house with dark green shutters. She had barely pulled on the parking brake when a large man, who seemed to come out of nowhere, rapped on her window. Both Jennifer and Teri jumped.

"What do you want?" he asked. Two hundred pounds easy. Maybe closer to three. And not a hair or a hat on his shaved head.

She rolled down the glass. “Jennifer Marsh. Mrs. Hovey is expecting me.”

The man took in her VW Bug and grunted, a bit like a disgruntled watchdog. The two women opened their doors and got out, but the man shook his head at Teri. “Only Marsh. Miz Hovey didn’t say nothin’ to me ’bout nobody else.”

Teri nodded at Jennifer. “That’s okay. You go ahead. I’ll be just fine. Out here in the cold. With more company than I’ve ever wanted.”

The man pointed toward the front of the house, and Jennifer followed a slate footpath around to a large, covered porch and an imposing, solid wood door with narrow, curtained windows running up and down each side of it. She pulled off her hat, stuffed it in her pocket, and quickly fluffed her hair. Then she rang the doorbell.

The curtains fluttered and then a woman with dark hair twisted into a bun opened the door. She appeared to be in her early forties and was dressed in an expensive angora turtleneck sweater and wool slacks. She bordered on plump, and the snug fit of her slacks made Jennifer suspect she was a yo-yo dieter.

"Miss Marsh. Won't you come in?"

A person can tell a lot about how someone has been brought up by her voice. This woman had class — genteel Southern class. Monied Southern class. And she knew exactly how to maintain politeness and show utter contempt at the same time. She even had coffee waiting in the living room, which was decorated in a hunting motif and filled with antiques. Over a gas fireplace hung a huge portrait of an older man with a mustache, wearing a suit with a vest and holding a pocket watch. Grandpa Loudermilk, Jennifer presumed.

Mrs. Hovey took Jennifer's coat, handed it to a servant, and then showed her to a sofa right out of the Ethan Allen catalogue. She offered to pour from the coffee service, but Jennifer shook her head.

"Fine. I like a woman who gets down to business. I believe you have some information for me," Ruth said, settling on the edge of the opposite love seat.

This was going to be more difficult than Jennifer had thought. This woman was stone hard under that delicate veneer. "Your husband, Richard Hovey . . . the night he died . . . he was waiting for someone. . . ."

Jennifer watched Ruth's gaze take in

every crease of her jeans and sweatshirt, every bit of grime on her hiking boots. She really should have gone home and dressed before she'd come. And done something about the hat hair that Teri had mentioned.

"Just what is it you're trying to say?" Ruth hadn't carried her age as well as her husband, and Jennifer knew immediately why her marriage had failed. Her own mother had told her more than once, "Never marry a man who's more attractive than you are. You'll never have a moment's peace. Women will always be hitting on him when you're out together, and you'll always wonder where he is when he's not with you." Good advice for the insecure. And good advice for Ruth Hovey. She looked as though she'd never had a moment's peace.

And Jennifer was about to disturb what little peace she may have found since Richard's death. She took a deep breath. "There were rose petals, burning candles, and a bottle of wine in Richard's bedroom the night he died. He was waiting for a woman. Mrs. Hovey —"

"How much?" she asked, her eyes rock hard, picking up a pen and checkbook off an end table.

Jennifer squinted at her. "How much what?"

Ruth stared at her with scorn. "We can do this easily or not, but I will not play games. I know that my husband could be a bottom feeder. He liked trash on occasion, but not as a steady diet. Whatever relationship you had with him —"

"Me?" Jennifer blushed as it struck her. Of course. Ruth sincerely believed Richard had not been waiting for Suzanne the night he died. Indeed, she thought Jennifer was that woman, the one he had strewn rose petals for, and that she was there to blackmail her into keeping the relationship quiet, no doubt so their children wouldn't find out their father had set a seduction scene the night he died.

"No. I never. I didn't even know Richard, Mr. Hovey, I mean. I never met him, never ever."

"You look like his type. Not too short. Young. Fairly attractive. You look like you'd clean up well. Too thin." The last two words came out with an inordinate amount of disdain.

She noted that Suzanne Gray did not fit that description.

But Kelli Byers did. More or less.

"You must be wondering how I know

about the rose petals. I have contacts with the press. I can certainly understand your wanting to keep what happened quiet. I do, too."

"Which brings us back to how much it will take to ensure your silence."

"No, no. I really do just want to know who Richard —" Darn! "— Mr. Hovey expected that night."

"And you think I know." She laughed.

"I thought you might at least have a guess."

"And what business is it of yours?"

"Mrs. Hovey, I'm working with Sam Culpepper."

"I know Mr. Culpepper. He's writing a book about Richard."

"Yes. I'm helping him with it. It seems that your husband's death or at least that of Suzanne Gray —"

"Don't mention that woman's name in this house." Ruth drew herself up. It was a challenge, one that Jennifer didn't dare take. "You should understand, Miss Marsh, that whatever sideshow Ms. Gray was putting on for the public had nothing whatsoever to do with my husband."

"I do understand that you believe that."

"It's not a matter of belief. It's a matter of fact. Do we understand one another?"

That Ruth Hovey was used to seeing to it that "fact" was what she said it was? Oh, yes. Jennifer understood perfectly.

"But if you truly believe it wasn't . . . that woman . . . who Richard was waiting for, you must have some guess who he was meeting that night."

"I don't. The only thing I'm certain of is that he wasn't waiting for Suzanne Gray."

"How can you be so sure?"

"Did you ever see Suzanne?"

"No, but —"

"She wasn't his type. Young women were always flocking around Richard. Put a man on TV or in the newspaper and women just can't resist him it seems. Young beautiful women."

"But they were engaged."

Ruth's eyes narrowed. The steel was back. She called out "Emily," and a woman in uniform appeared. "Would you please ask Burt to come in and show Miss Marsh out."

Jennifer was immediately on her feet. She was all too certain who Burt was. "That's quite all right. I'm sorry. Really. I didn't mean to offend you."

Mrs. Hovey opened her mouth to speak to Emily again, but Jennifer rushed on.

"I'm leaving. It was nice to meet you, Mrs. Hovey."

She'd probably just blown any chance of Ruth's cooperation with Sam. And he was going to kill her. But not before he made her very sorry.

Jennifer grabbed her coat from Emily and was out the door and down the front steps before Ruth had a chance to tell her again.

So that's where the belligerence came from. Ruth could accept losing Richard to a younger woman, but not to someone like Suzanne Gray, a woman close to her own age who was a good size twelve. Not to someone so like Ruth herself.

And she'd found out one very important piece of information: whoever Richard was expecting that night, it wasn't Ruth.

She scooted around to the side of the house. Teri was sitting on the driver's side of Jennifer's Bug, the motor running. Burt leaning against the door, talking to her through the window.

Jennifer slipped into the passenger seat.

"Nice to meet you. Gotta go," Teri said. The car groaned as Teri threw the transmission into reverse and then backed up. She scraped the gear back into first.

"Geez. You're tearing my transmission

apart. Since when did you drive a stick shift?" Jennifer asked.

"Since never."

"That second pedal down there is what's called a clutch. Push it in when you change gears."

The car lurched forward and the engine almost died.

"The clutch!" Jennifer hollered.

"Where's second?"

"Down and to your left."

Teri dragged the stick shift into gear and somehow got the little car going. It took off forward.

"It would be easier if you'd just let me drive."

"It would have been easier if you hadn't left me with Burt. He's a bad man."

At the end of the drive, Jennifer popped her door open and ordered Teri out. Instead, she climbed across the gearshift and the parking brake. Jennifer dashed around the car and slid under the wheel, and they took off down the main road as fast as flooring the gas pedal would allow.

"What do you mean he's a bad man?"

"He killed a guy. At least one. Hovey got him off."

"So what's he doing working for Ruth?"

"Hovey told him to. She needed someone, and, as best as I can tell, he's reliable."

"Only . . ."

"He moonlights. And I think he likes me." Teri's eyes grew huge. "He told me if I ever needed a job done, just let him know."

"What kind of job?"

"I didn't even want to ask."

Chapter 17

So where was he? Jennifer drummed her fingers against the tabletop and looked at her watch. Twelve-fifteen. She'd practically broken her neck to get to the restaurant on time and Sam was nowhere to be seen. She'd already been stood up by that man once this week and it was only Tuesday. The little storefront Bookstore Café was only a couple of blocks up from the *Telegraph* offices. He had no possible excuse.

Unless Belle had pulled something else. She'd like to bell that Belle, so she could keep track of her. She was turning Jennifer into a paranoid shrew, and Jennifer knew better than to let her do it. Of course Mrs. Walker and her *Men are weak, dear* wasn't helping either.

She fluffed at her hair. A good brushing had done little to help it, not with the static electricity in the air. At least she was dressed in something decent, gray slacks and a baby blue chenille turtleneck, a great improvement over the sweatshirt that Ruth

Hovey had seen her in.

She took a sip of water for the fifteenth time and glanced toward the windows flanking the door. Between the checked café curtains and the posters advertising poetry readings taped all over the inside of the windows, she could barely see the sunlight outside.

She didn't know why she was so anxious for Sam to get there. She wasn't looking forward to explaining to him what had happened at Ruth Hovey's. But he would simply have to understand that she'd only been trying to help. She replayed in her head what she planned to say to him. It was kind of a good news/bad news kind of thing. *I found out for sure that Ruth Hovey was not the woman Richard was expecting the night he died, but she'll probably never speak to either one of us again.* That would not go over well. How about, *Guess what? Ruth Hovey has this goon working for her but he only scared Teri. . . .* No. He wouldn't like that one either.

The door jingled. It was Sam. He looked harried. And not one bit happy. His gaze darted around the little place and then settled on her, back in the classic mystery section. She waved, trying to look relaxed. He came toward her, pulled off his coat, and dumped it in the spare chair at the table.

"He's definitely in Macon," Sam said.

"No, Sam. You mean DeSoto?"

He nodded.

"You think he's the one who trashed Belle's apartment."

"Yep."

"And that he's still looking for her?"

"I know he is. He was at the *Atlanta Eye* offices asking about her yesterday morning."

"You're kidding." A chill shot through her. Maybe Belle actually was in danger. Which meant Sam might be, too.

"He wasn't at all pleased when he was told she hadn't been in to work yesterday."

"But why do you think he's here?"

"Trainer's taking over his case. He's one of Hovey's partners. I dropped by their offices this morning. There was a news crew there waiting, which means they're sure to move the meeting off-site, but my bet is it still will be here in Macon."

"You don't happen to have a photo. . . ."

He pulled one out of his jacket pocket and handed it to her. "Actually, I have several. That's why I'm late. I had trouble getting the color printer to work. Take a good look. I don't want you approaching him if he shows up. Call the police. No, don't.

They couldn't do anything, unless he does something first. Call me. Don't talk to him. Just get the hell out."

She'd seen DeSoto's likeness in the newspaper and on TV, but she wanted to make sure she knew exactly what he looked like. He appeared tame enough in the photo, almost nerdish. His hair was dark and curly, and he wore thick-rimmed black glasses. Pretty harmless looking, really. But then they said Ted Bundy was a handsome dude.

A waitress shoved plastic-sleeved menus at them. Jennifer ordered the grilled red pepper and portobello mushroom sandwich from the "Today's Specials" clipped inside, not that she was particularly hungry, not anymore. Sam settled for an upscale version of a Philly cheesesteak.

"Did you find out anything at Hovey's office?" Jennifer asked.

"They wouldn't talk to me about DeSoto, of course. Attorney-client privilege. The receptionist did say Suzanne Gray sometimes called Hovey at the office, but he didn't like being disturbed at work."

Jennifer nodded. Or having his staff and coworkers privy to his personal life, she suspected. Surely they all knew and most likely had socialized with his ex-wife.

"I went by to see Ruth Hovey," she confessed.

Sam took a sip of her water. "Why?"

"Don't get mad. I simply asked if she knew who Richard was waiting for the night he died."

"But you already know Suzanne —"

"She doesn't think it was Suzanne."

Sam cocked an eyebrow at her. "She thinks Hovey was seeing another woman?"

"Yes. But she doesn't know who."

He waited for her to go on.

"She thought it was me. She thought I was there to shake her down."

"Ah, geez, Jennifer." He shook his head.

"It's all right," she assured him. "I explained that . . . actually I didn't tell her anything except that I didn't know her husband."

"Did she believe you?"

"I'm sure she did. I didn't take the check. That had to convince her. Lord only knows how much money she was willing to pay me to keep it quiet. Sam, are you sure Hovey never mentioned anything about a woman to you at all? I know not by name, but could he have alluded to Suzanne in some way?"

"Not that I remember. I'll have to check my tapes."

"Or maybe Kelli Byers?"

"Why would he mention that woman?"

"Teri and I were at the graveyard this morning and —"

"What the heck were you doing —"

Again, the bell jangled on the door and Jennifer looked up. Saved by the bell. Heck, *the* Belle. And she looked like hell, flustered, her face red and not just from the cold. She headed straight for their table.

"Someone's broken into . . ." she took a deep breath. "Sam, I got back to your apartment, and the lock was broken . . . I . . ."

Sam was immediately on his feet. Belle put her arms around him, burying her face against his chest. Gently he grasped her shoulders and pushed her back. "What's going on?"

"Your apartment. Sam. What if it was DeSoto? What if he . . ."

Sam grabbed his coat off the chair. "Jennifer, you stay here with Belle."

"No," Belle insisted. "I'm coming with you. Sam, I'm scared."

"Then why didn't you go to the police?" Jennifer muttered.

"What?" Sam asked.

"I said, why don't we go to the police?"

"They won't be able to help," Belle insisted. "There's nothing to tie DeSoto to anything that's happened."

"There's you," Jennifer said.

"No!" Belle shrieked.

Sam put an arm around her and shuffled her toward the door, leaving Jennifer to deal with the waitress who had miraculously appeared with both their orders. She pulled her last twenty out of her wallet and laid it on the table, and without a word followed after them.

Fuming, Jennifer brought up the tail end of their caravan to Sam's apartment, her fingers cramping around the steering wheel. Whatever danger Belle was in had just spilled into Jennifer's world, and she didn't like it one bit, especially all that hugging and comforting that went with it.

And as far as Jennifer was concerned, Belle no longer had any right to call the shots, not when Sam's personal safety and that of his property were involved.

Sam led the way into his parking area. He pulled his Honda into a space in front, and then Belle snatched the last space with her Miata. Jennifer had to go all the way down to the end and park in the row facing the street. They were waiting on the steps when she finally arrived, looking for all the world like a couple — Belle standing right up next to Sam, her hand resting on his chest, his arm, once again, around her.

They trudged up the stairs, no one saying a word, and finally got a look at the damage. The door frame was splintered at the lock.

"Looks like they used a crowbar. On hundred-year-old wood. Why didn't they just kick in the damn door? Did you go inside?" Sam asked Belle.

She nodded.

"You know better," he chastised her.

"I do. I'm sorry. I panicked."

Really? Panic in Jennifer's book meant to run away, not run toward.

Sam barely touched the door and it swung inward. The room looked normal, as though it hadn't been touched. He motioned for them to stay put, while he slipped into the bedroom, then the bath, and finally the kitchen. He came back into the living room shaking his head. "I don't get it."

"I know," Belle agreed. "Nothing's been touched, except. . . ."

"Except what?" Jennifer asked.

"My things. In the bedroom. They . . ."

"Someone dumped Belle's bags all over the bed. Did you notice anything missing?"

Belle shook her head.

"Then why?" Jennifer asked.

"My guess is to see who they belonged to," Sam said.

Belle nodded. She looked as if she was near tears. She seemed to be blinking and swallowing a lot.

"I need something to drink," Belle announced. Then she disappeared into the kitchen.

"Check your desk," Jennifer ordered as soon as Belle was out of earshot.

"Why?" Sam asked.

"This wasn't a burglary. You're assuming DeSoto was here, hoping to find Belle or at least to make sure she was staying here. Whatever. You're probably right. But check your files. It's no secret that Hovey had asked you to collaborate on his book. DeSoto may want to make sure no client privilege was broken, that you don't know something that might hurt his new trial."

Sam went to his desk and dug into the bottom drawer. He pulled out a manila envelope and shook it. Nothing. Then he drew out a folder and held it up. It, too, was empty. Jennifer peered over his shoulder. *Richard Hovey* was written across both the envelope and the tab of the folder.

"He got the tapes and the notes," Sam stated.

"What's going on out there?" Belle called from the kitchen. She came out drinking straight from a carton of orange juice.

Jennifer dashed into the kitchen and came back with a glass. She snatched the carton from Belle, poured her a cup, and handed it to her.

"Getting all formal on me?" Belle noted, seeming far more composed than she'd been a minute ago. "Sam drinks from the carton."

Oh, yuck. Could this get more icky? Of course it could.

"What are you doing?" Belle asked Sam, looking over his shoulder.

"My notes and the interviews with Hovey seem to be missing."

"Then it must have been DeSoto," Belle said. "He knows I'm here, and he knows about the work you did with Hovey."

Sam already had his computer on and was searching his files. "Okay. They got the computer files, too. Then deleted them off the hard drive."

"You're kidding." Jennifer set the juice carton on the coffee table and was immediately at Sam's side, staring over his other shoulder at the screen. "Sam, all that work. And now Hovey's dead. . . . Did they get anything else?"

Sam shook his head. "Not that I can tell."

"Bummer!" Belle declared, pouring herself another glass of juice.

Sam pulled out the bottom desk drawer and drew out a box of unlabeled disks. He took one from the back and held it up. "It pays to back up your work." Then he slipped the disk into the machine, pulled up the files, and copied them onto another disk.

"Here," he said, giving the copy to Jennifer. "Hang onto this for me." Then he slipped the original disk into his pocket.

Jennifer let out her breath. "What could be in these files that anyone would want?"

"I have no idea." Sam switched off his computer and grabbed back up his coat. "You two, out."

Belle looked at him over her juice glass. "But I'm —"

"You heard me." He took the glass out of her hand and put it on the table. "Belle, you are now officially staying with Jennifer until further notice. I'm calling the police and I don't want you here when they arrive."

"At least let me get my clothes," Belle protested.

"Later," Sam said.

"But the police will know I've been staying here."

"Right. Because you have," Sam said.

"Are you going to tell them about DeSoto?"

"I don't know. They'll take fingerprints. His are in the database."

Then he pushed them both out the door.

They stood outside looking at each other.

"Okay, roomie," Belle said, "I'll need a key to your place, unless you plan for us to be attached at the hip."

Right. Her fondest desire. Jennifer headed toward her car.

"And you need to know I shower in the mornings," Belle called after her, "and I —"

"Follow me." Jennifer climbed into her car. If there was a motel room to be had in Macon, Georgia, she was going to see to it that Belle slept in it that night.

Chapter 18

Why would anyone in their right mind schedule a convention of Jehovah's Witnesses in the middle of February in Macon? The guy at the front desk of the Best Western on the way home from Sam's apartment told Jennifer she might as well hang it up. It seemed as if all of them, plus a few spares, had booked every bed from the Quality Inn to the Hilton through at least Saturday. Belle wasn't getting a room until they finished their weeklong convention at the coliseum. Or she converted, whichever came first.

Somebody better find that DeSoto dude and soon.

Reluctantly, Jennifer led Belle on to the hardware store on Riverside and, a few minutes later, with freshly minted key in hand, unlocked the door to her apartment.

"No room at the inn, huh," Belle declared as they came in the door.

Jennifer grunted, and Muffy had a new-person-to-play-with fit, displaying truly atrocious, bad-dog manners. It brought a naughty smile to Jennifer's lips.

"Could you tell her I don't like dogs?" Belle asked, shoving Muffy off her for the second time.

"Better let her lick you," Jennifer warned. "You want to let her get to know you. She's a guard dog." Well, she was, sort of. Just a sweet, well-meaning guard dog.

Belle screwed up her face and allowed Muffy to slobber all over her hands. "Is this really necessary?"

"Oh, I think so."

Jennifer tossed the new key on the table. "Okay, that one's yours. Make sure you lock the door each time you leave and each time you come in. Don't drink from anything in my apartment except a glass. Wash up after you use any dishes; there's one of those sponges with the liquid soap in it next to the sink. You're welcome to whatever I have in the fridge, but be forewarned this is a vegetarian household. Oh, and I shower first in the mornings. No using my shower cap."

When Jennifer paused, she saw Belle wiping her hands on the back of her pants. Muffy had lost all interest and was pouting. She, too, had discovered that Belle was no fun.

"You can sleep in my bedroom. You'll find fresh sheets in the hall closet." It galled her to give Belle her bed, but she wasn't about to leave her in the living room with her computer. "I go to sleep at eleven, so I'd appreciate it if you did, too, or at least if you would quietly retire to your room by then."

"Anything else?"

"Oh, I'm sure I'll think of several elses, but right now I've got something I've got to do." And with that, Jennifer headed right back out the door. Belle would be safe while Jennifer took care of a little business that was begging to be finished, and Sam had said nothing about not letting Belle out of her sight.

"I wanted to let you know Sam took the black dress to the medical examiner's office," Jennifer said.

Marjorie held open the screen door and waved her inside as she dried her hands on a dish towel. "You've caught me on the tail end of washing up the lunch dishes. Vic was late getting in today. One of the cows got her head caught in some barbed wire, and he like to never got her out. I may have some coffee left. Want some?"

Jennifer shook her head. It wouldn't do

well on an empty stomach. "Thanks but I'm all right."

"Suzie!" Marjorie sang out. "That girl was here just a moment ago. Turned my back to open the door and off she went. She was supposed to do some laundry for me. Well, that can wait until after you're gone. Is there something else I can do for you?"

"I just wondered if you'd received Suzanne's belongings."

"About nine o'clock this morning. All neatly folded, like they were ready for her to shake out and hang back up." Marjorie shook her head and swatted at her eyes with her dishcloth.

"Did you recognize the dress?" That's really why Jennifer had come by, in hopes of getting a look.

"Oh, yes. It's the one I thought it was. She wore it all the time, only during the summer. It's way too cold for it now. She always looked like an angel in it. You want to see it?"

Jennifer nodded.

Marjorie led her down a narrow hall to a small back bedroom. "When she sang in church in the summertime, she'd usually put it on." She pulled open the drapes. The items were laid out on the single bed.

The dress, the gloves. In a small plastic bag were small pearl earrings, an anklet with a tiny enameled bird hanging from it, the blue ribbon, and a watch with a bracelet band. Her hose and underwear were in another. Her shoes in a third. The note in yet one more.

"Is this all the jewelry she was wearing?" Jennifer asked. "Hadn't Richard given her an engagement ring?"

"None that I ever saw, but they were keeping things quiet. What with the reaction I got from his family, I imagine he was smart enough not to stir up any trouble until after they'd actually tied the knot."

Jennifer picked up the bag with the shoes in it. Slick and clean as if they'd just come out of the box. Not a scuff mark on either one. "Do you recognize these?"

Marjorie shook her head. "But I know where she bought them. They'd be a special order. Nine wide. I already checked the size. Those people who carry those kind of shoes in the stores figure a person don't much care if they're a little uncomfortable for the short time you'll wear them, but Suzanne had to have hers wide. She wouldn't settle for nothing else."

Jennifer touched the bag with the jewelry. "What about this anklet?"

"Is that what it is? I thought it was a bracelet."

"Do you recognize it?"

Marjorie shook her head.

"I don't suppose you'd consider letting me borrow it?"

"Take it. I don't want the thing. I was thinking about throwing all of it out, but I know Suzie would have a fit. She's not good at letting go, but I can't bear to look at any of it. Maybe when she goes off to work tonight —"

"Don't throw Suzanne's things away," Jennifer warned her, slipping the anklet into her pants pocket. "I'll be glad to pack it if you've got a box. You could put it in the back of a closet, where you don't have to look at it."

She picked up the bag with the note in it. It was creased, of course, from where it had been folded but it lay open in the bag, easily read through the plastic.

Richard, I can't live without you. You're my life, my love, my death.

To whoever finds my body, let me find the peace in death that eluded me in life. Do not desecrate my body with an autopsy. Do not bury me, but scatter my ashes to the winds so I can become part of this earth and its promise of new life.

Suzanne Gray

Interesting. Richard got hardly more than a line. The disposal of Suzanne's body, more than three times as much. And her name was typed right up next to the last line, leaving no room for a signature.

"We met Kelli Byers last night," Jennifer said, looking up.

Marjorie shook her head. "I should have warned you about her. She lives just across the street, and I swear, she spends more time staring out that window than doing any of her own business. I hope she didn't embarrass you much."

"She called the cops on us. She thought we'd broken in."

"I know and I apologize. I had no idea she'd pull some fool stunt like that. Guess I should have called her and let her know you all were going down there, but the whole idea was to keep her out of it."

As if Kelli was about to allow that to happen.

"Did they return Suzanne's coat?"

"What coat?" Marjorie asked.

"I thought there might have been a winter coat left at the scene or in Suzanne's car."

"Her car's here. Vic put it out in the shed, but there wasn't any coat in it."

"And no shoes, I'll wager," Jennifer said, more to herself than to anyone else.

"I showed you her shoes already." Marjorie lifted the bag with the satin shoes.

"Right," Jennifer agreed. "And the flowers she was holding. What happened to them?"

"They gave them back to us, all right. Can you imagine, like they were something anybody might want? Vic threw them out in the trash can outside."

"You mind if I take a look before I leave?"

"If you want to go messin' around in my garbage, I suppose it's all right so long as you clean up after yourself. Why are you so all-fired interested in all this anyway? I tell you what you should be doing and that's realizing that Sam Culpepper has quite a thing for you. He may be living with that other woman, although I can't imagine what he sees in her excepting maybe the package she's wrapped in, but, honey, I saw the way he looked at you. I'd stake my money that it's you he's crazy about."

Jennifer blushed, almost down to her toes. She could have kissed Marjorie right then and there.

"Find me that box and I'll pack Suzanne's things for you," Jennifer promised.

"All right. But you listen up to what I just told you. More times than not, it's us women who do the deciding for men. You even think you might someday want that Sam Culpepper, you'd better consider it now because that Belle woman has an agenda all laid out for him."

And if it was that obvious to a complete stranger, why was it that Sam couldn't see it?

"I'll be back in just a minute. I think I have something we can use out on the back porch."

Jennifer looked about the room. Faded flowered wallpaper, the single bed with a solid blue coverlet, an old photo of a couple, and another of a young Suzanne and a small child, Suzie, on either side of the single window. A small bookcase with worn books and stuffed toys. A dusty crystal box on the bedside table. This must have once been Suzanne's room.

"Will this do?" Marjorie asked from the doorway. She offered a plain brown, open-ended cardboard box.

"How long did she live with you?" Jennifer asked, accepting the box.

"From her second year of high school up

until about ten years ago. She needed to get her own life. That's why Vic built her that house. And Vic and I, we needed our space. Suzie, too. She was soon to be starting her teen years, and we had our own ideas about how she ought to be reared. But now I wonder if things might have been different if we'd kept Suzanne with us."

Seems every time someone died, there was always more guilt to go around than people to absorb it.

Jennifer folded the dress and carefully laid it in the box. Then she added the shoes and the other bags.

Marjorie opened the closet door and used her foot to shove shoes and boots to one side. "You can put it in here."

Jennifer set it on the floor, noting that Marjorie seemed reluctant to touch a single item, not even the box. "Don't blame yourself. Things happen. It's not as though you could have done anything to prevent it."

Marjorie looked into her eyes. "But I saw it coming. What happened with that Lewis Spikes boy and then with Vic. I saw it coming."

Chapter 19

Unfortunately, the guilt-ridden don't necessarily feel obligated to unburden their souls, and Marjorie didn't share another word. She simply showed Jennifer the door and left her guessing what she might mean.

She found Suzanne's roses, or what was left of them, in the trash, thankfully on top. Definitely thorned.

Jennifer rewrapped the roses in the brown paper she'd found them in and stowed them in the trunk of her car. As she pushed the lid shut, she heard "Jennifer." She turned to see Suzie standing directly behind her.

"I wondered where you were."

"Did Mama show you Aunt Suzanne's things?"

"Yes. I packed them for her."

"Did you see the anklet?"

Jennifer dug it out of her pocket. "She let me take it with me."

"It's not Aunt Suzanne's," Suzie said confidently.

"Do you know who it belongs to?"

Suzie shook her head. "It's not Kelli's either. At least I've never seen her wear it and I've seen most of what that woman owns. It's her something borrowed. That's what you thought, too, isn't it? Her killer planted it on her."

"Is that what you think?"

"Of course."

"This is the first time I've heard you use the word *killer.* Before you just said Suzanne didn't kill herself."

"Sometimes it's wise to let someone warm up to an idea. I didn't want to scare you off."

"Learned that from your mama, huh?"

"Oh, yeah, from dealing with my mama. And my dad."

"But Suzanne could have gotten that anklet from anywhere, or bought it herself in the store. I really don't think we can put too much stock in —"

"Look at it." She took the jewelry out of Jennifer's hand. "It's worn. See? One of the wings on the little bird has lost its sharp corner, probably from beating against the side of a shoe. Besides, Aunt Suzanne already had her something borrowed, a tiny gold locket. She gave it to me on my sixteenth birthday and I gave it back to her about a month ago to keep until the ceremony. It's down at her house. I can show you, if you don't believe me."

"Of course, I believe you, Suzie. Why wouldn't I?"

"Jennifer, whoever killed her knew all about her plans to marry Mr. Hovey. That's why she was dressed up like she was. What they didn't know was how to lay her out right, how Aunt Suzanne herself would have done it."

It gave her little shivers hearing how this young woman would know how her aunt would have committed suicide. She glanced back toward the house and saw Marjorie watching them from the window. The moment she realized Jennifer was looking, she drew back.

What, Jennifer wondered, had happened between Vic and Suzanne that made them decide they had to get her out of the house?

When she got home, Muffy didn't even stir at the sound of the key in the door. She was snuggled at Belle's side. On the sofa. Where she was never, ever supposed to be.

"Muffy is not allowed on the furniture," Jennifer stated firmly. The dog bounced down and slunk off toward the bedroom, fully aware of her unacceptable behavior.

"Too bad, Muff. Big bad mama is home," Belle said. "So, how's it going? Where were you?"

"No place you need to know about. Any calls?"

"Not a one. Oh, except for Sam checking up on us. The police had left and he was waiting for the repairman. We had a nice, long conversation. He wanted to know where you were."

"And where is he?"

"Right now? Probably out looking for DeSoto."

"Please tell me you're kidding. You actually let him —"

"Hey, I didn't have anything to do with it. Sam's a big boy, Jennifer, if you hadn't noticed."

Oh, she'd noticed all right.

"If he calls back and I'm gone, you tell him to call me at Monique's. Or on my cell phone. Tell him I turned it on. You got that?"

"Sure. Monica whatever."

"Monique Dupree." She found a sticky note and a pen, wrote Monique's name down, and tossed the pad at her. "Don't forget."

"Okay, okay."

She slipped into her tiny kitchen and pulled a frozen pizza-for-one out of the freezer. Then she ripped it out of its box and slapped it into the microwave. She poured herself a Coke and chugged down half of it. As soon as the timer sounded, she choked down the pizza, standing right there, leaning up against the counter.

"Oh, Jennifer," Belle sang out. "When you get finished in the kitchen, you might want to check out your mail. The mailman brought it up. A thick manila envelope. Looks self-addressed. It's got a New York postmark. I laid it on your desk."

Great. Just when she thought her life couldn't get any worse, some New York publisher decided to put the cherry on the sundae and send one of her manuscripts back. And Belle was right there to bear witness.

Chapter 20

"You're kidding. That woman is not staying in your home." Leigh Ann crossed her arms, offered Jennifer a most disgusted look, and tilted back in her chair in Monique's spacious kitchen.

"Even as we speak," Jennifer assured her and the rest of the gang, pulling a chair up to the table. "She's probably drinking right out of my milk carton and eating all my chocolate doughnuts."

"Better to keep the fox out of the chicken coop," April declared, "even if that means taking him into your own home." She helped herself to a piece of Mississippi Mud, a gooey chocolate brownie, melted-marshmallow, chocolate-icing concoction that should come with a sugar-shock warning, as should most everything April baked. "Anyone got any ideas about how to get rid of this Belle woman?"

She shoved the pan across the table toward Leigh Ann who immediately cut a huge piece. Someday her calorie count had to catch up with the skinny little thing. At least that's what April always said.

Monique cleared her throat, and they all turned to look as she leaned back against the counter. "How can we help? I have a spare room."

Jennifer was truly touched. "No, that's all right. Actually I kind of like having Belle where I can watch her. What I really need help with is finding out what was going on with Suzanne Gray."

"I don't see the point in that," April said, savoring the rich chocolate on her tongue. "I mean this poor Suzanne Gray woman is dead, and so is the man she threw herself away for. There's no helping either one of them, but Jennifer and Sam, now, the two of them need a good bit of help. We can do something about their situation."

"Excuse me?" Jennifer interrupted. A little sympathy was just fine. Meddling was a whole other matter. "Suzanne Gray deserves justice, dead or alive."

"Just lay it on us," Teri declared. "She's not going to let this one go, you all. So what do you need to know?"

"Who killed Suzanne Gray, for starters."

"That's for enders," Leigh Ann declared, shuffling the brownie pan toward Teri. "But for my money, she offed herself. Lost love. How could you doubt it?"

Monique set a gallon milk jug in the middle of the table. "You said yourself the woman was determined to be wed before her fortieth birthday." She grabbed some glasses and poured milk for everyone, not bothering to ask whether they wanted it or not. Women need calcium.

"Yeah, so why didn't Richard Hovey's parents know about the wedding plans?" Jennifer asked.

Leigh Ann's brow creased. "You're right. They should have. Even if they hated her."

"You're kidding," Teri threw in. "That man was forty-two years old and a gazillionaire. He didn't have to tell his parents a thing."

"What about all that stuff you said you and Sam found in her house?" April asked. "All those wedding preparations. I can't imagine anyone going to all that trouble and being able to keep a secret like that."

"Right. That's where you all come in," Jennifer stated. If they were all so anxious to help, then she'd let them. "We know Suzanne and Richard's engagement announcement, modest though it was, appeared in the newspaper, but without a set date. I want to know exactly how far the wedding arrangements had progressed. The dress swatches came from La Boutique Nuptiale. I'll check it out. If she actually ordered a dress, put down money, I want to know. And when it was to be delivered. I have no idea how long it takes to have a gown made —"

"Months," April broke in. "Especially when you add the fittings. It usually takes at least two."

"That's what I thought."

"And then there are the dresses for the attendants," Leigh Ann threw in.

"Right. Got it covered," Jennifer went on. "The jewelry brochures were from Astor's. Surely Richard Hovey would buy one whopping ring for his bride-to-be, even if it's never been found. Leigh Ann, you like rings. You take that one."

"I like dresses, too," she pouted under her breath.

"The stationery samples came from Pastorelli's. Don't you know them, Monique?" Jennifer asked.

Monique nodded. "I'll get on it in the morning."

"The flowers from Carmichael's —"

"I'll take that one," Teri offered.

"I'll check out the bakery," April volunteered. No big surprise there.

"Okay. That's Lazy Susan's."

"Got it."

"That only leaves Talley's Travels."

"I'll take that one, too," Monique offered.

"Terrific. I guess that about covers it, at least for now," Jennifer said.

"So what is it we want to know exactly?" Leigh Ann asked.

"What Suzanne and Richard ordered. If they actually put down deposits. When they did it, what date they gave for the wedding, etc."

"And you think this will help you understand her death?" Monique still didn't seem convinced.

"Either these two people were madly in love and Suzanne killed herself when Richard died —"

"That's so beautiful, isn't it?" Leigh Ann interrupted.

"No, it's not," Teri snapped.

"Either Suzanne killed herself," Jennifer went on, "or someone staged an awfully elaborate murder, someone who was aware of the wedding plans. I want to know which it was."

"Why?" Monique asked again. It wasn't a challenge, really. It was more a recognition that something more was going on with Jennifer. "I mean why all the detail?"

"I'm going to write about it."

"Oh," Leigh Ann said. "You mean you're going to use it as a basis for a novel."

"No. Teri already knows this. Sam and I are going to write a true crime book about Richard Hovey. I'm . . . I'm not going to write fiction anymore."

"I sure as heck didn't know that last part," Teri said.

None of the rest of them said a word. They sat there stunned.

"What happened?" Monique asked.

"I told you. This poor woman is crying out for justice and —"

"No. What happened to you? Did you finally hear back from that publisher about your Jolene Arizona book?"

She knew she should have burned that book. She should never have let anyone read it or know that she'd written it. But all those rejections she collected from all her other books, so many of them demanding something totally new, something never done before, had spurred her on. And so Jolene had been born, a left-handed, blind-in-one-eye, bareback-riding circus performer turned private eye, who slept with almost everybody on God's green earth. And, nine months ago, in a fit of weakness,

Jennifer had actually submitted it to a New York publisher.

"Yes, I heard back. This afternoon."

"Are you going to tell us what they said?" Monique asked, frozen, milk jug in hand.

"They said they really, really liked it, but they just bought a book very similar to it. They told me to try again." Jennifer fought the bile she felt rising in her throat. "Only they wanted more sex and more violence."

"That's terrific!" Leigh Ann clapped her hands.

"It's not terrific. It's disgusting. I'm done with fiction. I'd be done with writing only. . . ."

"We don't choose what we are," Monique told her. "You're either a writer or you're not, and you, Jennifer Marsh, are a writer."

They all paused for a moment. No one would press the issue. Not now. Jennifer was serious and they knew it.

And so was Monique.

"Okay. Everyone's got their assignments." Monique wisely said no more. "I want to see everybody back here tomorrow night so we can pool our information."

"That's awfully tight —" Teri complained.

"Just do it, Teri," April insisted, packing up what was left of the brownies. "So you lose a lunch hour or an hour after work. Jennifer won't let us move on to more important things until we do it, and every minute that Belle woman remains in her life —"

Jennifer was on her feet. "I'm going home." She grabbed her shoulder bag, but April managed to catch hold of the straps and pull her aside before she got to the door.

"We need to talk."

Jennifer stared at her.

"If my getting a contract for my Billy and Barney books has discouraged you in any way. . . ." April whispered.

She pulled her arm out of April's grasp. "I'm thrilled for you. Write your books. Publish two million of them. It's all good with me. You deserve it."

"I may deserve it, but you deserve it, too. I can't even imagine how you must feel after that awful letter about your Jolene Arizona book. You should never have sent that book out. You should never have written it."

"Thanks for sharing, but you don't understand today's adult fiction market. If you're going to lecture me on the morality of writing books that deal with sex and violence —"

"Go back to your first love, Jennifer. Your Maxie Malone books have come within a breath of selling. They're charming, they're witty, they're moral. Maxie's a strong female character that won't let anybody stop her. She's a lot like you. I know you can find someone to print them. You've had at least two encouraging replies from queries. You're getting close."

"Close only counts in horseshoes and hand grenades, certainly not in publishing."

"But you can't give up now," April insisted.

"Then just when can I give up?" Jennifer didn't want to cry in front of April or any of the rest of them. She was so tired her limbs were moving on their own and she had just about had it. "My social life is in shambles, Suzanne is dead in some undertaker's back room, Sam is God knows where doing who knows what, Belle has taken over my home, my money is running low, and it's so cold that I have only one catering job scheduled with Dee Dee and that's Friday when I'd much rather be out doing something with Sam. My writing is a lost cause, and —"

"It's always darkest just before the dawn," Leigh Ann offered, sweeping past them.

"Actually it's always darkest before it gets pitch-black," Teri pointed out as she pushed past and out the door. "See you all tomorrow."

And her writing group was dissolving into trite and catty backbiters. Okay, that wasn't fair. They'd always had their share of the trite and catty.

But as much as she loved April, one of the truly good people in this world, Jennifer couldn't bear to hear one more time how talented she was and how unfair it was that she wasn't published. "April, go home to your babies and Craig."

Jennifer then turned and left without another word. She had to get home to Muffy and check on that horrid woman Belle. What else could possibly go wrong?

Even as the thought entered her mind, she knew no one should ever pose that question, not even to oneself.

Chapter 21

Jennifer wasn't the only one whose life was tumbling out of control. Sam hadn't been home all last evening. She knew because, after she got back from her writers' group, she'd called his house several times and gotten no answer. Bright and early the next morning, he called her. She met him on the front steps of the Bibb County Courthouse.

"A restraining order? How did DeSoto get a judge to grant him an order against you?"

"Let's just say I got a little overly enthusiastic with my accusations. C'mon. I need coffee. We can get some at the canteen in the basement."

"Sam, you know better," she told him, following him past tall columns and into the building. "Obviously you must have found DeSoto."

He led her across the marble floor to the bank of elevators on the left and punched the down button. "Oh, I found him all right. But not until after the officer completed the report on the break-in at my apartment and I called someone to fix my door. Do you know that frame is over a hundred years old? Do you have any idea how much money it's going to cost to repair it? It has to meet historic specifications, with salvaged wood. Can you even guess how hard that is to find?"

"Okay, okay," Jennifer soothed, trying to look inconspicuous as two men in business suits, both carrying briefcases, joined them to wait for the elevator. "You got the repairman over. Then what?"

"I went back to Hovey's offices."

"You didn't."

The elevator door slid open and all four of them stepped inside.

"The police weren't going to do anything," Sam told her. "Nothing was damaged except the door frame. Nothing was missing except my files. You know where that puts the incident on the priority list."

"Did the police ask you about Belle?"

"Not a word. Only if anything was stolen."

"So you got to the law offices. . . ."

"And I waited around out back, along the only street with open parking, and I confronted DeSoto when he slipped out the back to get into his car."

"Great. Were his attorneys with him?"

"Only Trainer. He called the police."

"Oh, no, Sam. They arrested you?"

"Not exactly. But I had to show up in court this morning."

The elevator thunked to a stop and the doors opened again. Jennifer stepped out and turned to see one of the suited men pass Sam a business card. She caught something about "needing an attorney."

Sam thanked him and slipped the card into his pocket, then waited for the man to disappear down the hall. "Great place to pick up clients. Roam the halls of the courthouse."

"He's right, you know," Jennifer chastised him. "You should have had a lawyer with you. I can't believe the judge actually granted the order against you. He must have determined you were a danger to DeSoto."

"The man invaded my home."

"A danger to him, not to you, Sam. And you don't know for certain it was DeSoto," Jennifer whispered as they swung through the door into the small canteen area. "You can't go around claiming —"

"Were you listening in when the judge lectured me?"

Calm, cool, Sam. The very soul of logic,

until someone invaded his personal space. And threatened people that he cared about.

"How did he react?"

"The judge was not pleased."

"No, I mean DeSoto. What did he do when you yelled at him?"

"He was indignant. Furious. He used a few word combinations even I hadn't heard before."

"Picked those up in prison, I'd guess."

"Right. A hotbed for new vocabulary."

"What can I get for you?" the man behind the counter asked.

"Two coffees and . . ." he looked around the display. The only things to eat were prepackaged. "Got any sandwiches?"

"Sure, over in the refrigerator case." He pointed against the wall.

"Okay, I'll have a ham and —"

"They're all the same price. Just go pick one out."

"Okay, make that two whatevers. That okay with you?"

She nodded her head. She had to meet Leigh Ann during her lunch hour, and she wouldn't have a chance to grab anything else to eat.

The man poured the coffee into Styrofoam cups, capped them, and pushed them forward. Sam gave him a twenty and got his change, and they headed to the case. Ham and cheese for Sam. Egg salad for her. Then they found a tiny table in the back corner.

"Did you mention Belle?" Jennifer asked, slipping into a chair.

"Of course not. I gave DeSoto hell for my door. If there was even the remotest possibility that he wasn't the one who broke into my place, or that he hadn't figured out she'd been staying with me, I wasn't about to tell him."

At least he'd had enough wits about him not to tell all he knew. "Sam, you can't do this." She unwrapped her egg salad sandwich. She didn't even want to know when it was made.

"I know."

"Please. Promise me. If DeSoto is a killer . . . I couldn't bear for anything to happen to you."

"Don't worry about it. The judge says DeSoto and I are not to come within five hundred feet of each other."

And with a good rifle and a decent scope, that'd be plenty close enough.

Chapter 22

"The woman had good taste, I'll say that much for her," Leigh Ann said, touching the lace on a Gawain gown hanging at La Boutique Nuptiale. "Ooooh. They always look so cute in these tiny sizes," she declared, taking down a size-two wedding dress from the sample rack and holding it in front of her. Leigh Ann had insisted that she come along with Jennifer to look at dresses. As far as she was concerned, it was better than lunch any day.

When they'd arrived at the shop, the lone clerk had been busy at the register filling out an order with a young woman who looked to be still in high school. Leigh Ann had grabbed Jennifer and headed straight for the dresses.

"Don't you wish you could fit into this dress?" Leigh Ann gushed.

"No. My skeleton's bigger than that." Jennifer grabbed hold of the price tag. "And for what it costs, it should look stunning in a size eighteen. You didn't have to come along, you know."

"But I wanted the dress assignment. And it's not fun to look by yourself."

"We're not looking," Jennifer reminded her. "We're trying to find out if Suzanne Gray bought a wedding dress. That looks to be about your size."

Leigh Ann held the beaded, strapless, floor-length gown in shimmering satin in front of her. "My size? Oh, no. I wear a four. It's huge next to this one."

Must be all in the perspective.

"How long do you think the woman who wears this will stay a size two?" Leigh Ann asked.

"Until she has a piece of wedding cake."

"Had Suzanne pulled out a specific fabric sample?"

"Not that I could tell. Belle was all over everything."

"The nerve of that Belle woman. Why Sam ever let her step foot in his apartment —"

"He's a good guy. He does the knight-in-shining-armor thing well."

"You mean he's dumb about women."

"Yes, at least as far as this one goes."

"So you don't really have any idea what Suzanne might have selected."

"No, but the woman was almost forty.

You wouldn't expect her to choose something strapless."

"If I were choosing a wedding dress to freeze to death in, it'd be a full-length white velvet."

"And you'd accessorize it with a parka, which would defeat the whole purpose."

Leigh Ann grinned. "You know me so well. Actually I'd add one of those little bolero jackets trimmed in fake white fur, fake because I wouldn't want any animals harmed just so I could look good when I died and because I know you'd never let me hear the end of it. But then I'd be dead so I guess it wouldn't matter anyway. Oh, and I'd add a little pillbox entirely covered in matching fur. What was Suzanne wearing when they found her?"

"A simple white dress, gloves, her hair ribbon, a pair of panty hose, and her bra and panties. And shoes."

"No slip?"

"No."

"She'd need a slip to make the lines fall right. I'd have suggested one of those slimming all-in-ones with the bra built in. They do wonders," Leigh Ann assured her.

"She was just dressing to die," Jennifer reminded her.

"Precisely my point. It was the last impression. She would want to look good. From what you've said, she was doing it up right. Any jewelry?"

"Small pearl earrings."

"Classic. No engagement ring?"

"No. That is odd, isn't it?"

"Maybe she was afraid of its being stolen. Personally, I wouldn't kill myself for someone who hadn't even given me at least a two-carat diamond. What do you think of this one?" Leigh Ann asked, pulling from the rack a sleek off-one-shoulder gown in antique-colored silk. Its full, floor-length skirt was inset with lace panels that were accented with seed pearls.

"I think it's probably not what Suzanne would have selected," Jennifer reminded her.

"So that was all she had on? Everything they gave back to the sister? What does that do to your something-borrowed theory?"

"There was one other item. An anklet with a single charm, the only item Marjorie didn't recognize. And Suzie didn't know it either. Marjorie said Suzanne wore the earrings a lot."

"That would have been her something old," Leigh Ann suggested. "The anklet must have been her something borrowed.

You don't have anything else for it. I don't suppose she happened to have a handkerchief."

"No handkerchief. I've already given you the entire inventory."

Leigh Ann continued to paw through the racks. "What she was wearing, was it something like this?"

Jennifer turned. It was a straight street-length sheath, this one in satin, but suddenly she could see Suzanne standing there wearing it, drawing back her dark hair with that blue ribbon, a determined look on her face.

No, wait. If that were the case, it wouldn't have been murder and in her heart, she knew it was. Because in her mind's eye, she could see Suzanne, wearing that dress, sitting down, taking up a pen and, tears falling, writing her suicide note. Writing it, darn it, not typing the thing on a computer or some typewriter.

"We've got to talk to a salesclerk. You'd think with no more people in the store, the clerk would be all over us trying to help."

"Oh. That first woman left and now she's busy with some woman over there." Leigh Ann pointed and Jennifer looked past the rack to see the clerk in deep conversation. When the woman turned, Jennifer stood stunned. Belle Renard.

She was supposed to be lying low at Jennifer's apartment.

"Oh, my goodness," Leigh Ann squeaked. "Do you see who that is? You know Belle really is the perfect woman. Just look at her. All that curly reddish brown hair. Dimples. Great figure. Fabulous —"

"Stuff a sock in it. What's she doing here?"

"Oh, Jen, and you let her convince you the threat wasn't real. She's obviously looking for a dress for her wedding to Sam. You poor thing. I told you that woman plans to marry Sam."

Jennifer growled. She couldn't help it. "You did not and she is not. If I had to guess, I'd say she's here doing exactly what we're doing. But why?"

Leigh Ann peeked over a rack. "She's helping Sam, too, just like you are. Look, the saleswoman is shaking her head." Suddenly Leigh Ann disappeared among a fluff of fabric, and Jennifer felt a hand grab her, dragging her in with her. "She's coming this way." They peeked through the lace, watching Belle walk dangerously close and then out through the front entrance. A little bell signaled her exit.

"If Belle is so terrified of Simon DeSoto, what the heck is she doing here, wandering around in broad daylight?" Leigh Ann whispered.

"Can I help you ladies?" The clerk stared down at them, none too pleased.

"Yes, you can." Jennifer tried to find some dignity as she untangled herself from lace and satin. She grabbed Leigh Ann's arm and jerked her upright.

"Does Suzanne Gray have a dress on order for a June wedding?"

"How odd. A woman was just in here asking if anyone had been inquiring about the same account. I'll tell you what I told her. We keep our customers' purchases confidential. If you were getting married, I'm certain you wouldn't want us to divulge information about your gown."

"I don't suppose if I said that you could tell anyone who asks about my buying habits, that you'd tell me about this one."

The clerk smiled and shook her head. "Suzanne Gray. That name sounds awfully familiar."

"That's right," Leigh Ann jumped in. "She has the same name as the woman who killed herself in the cemetery. Isn't that awful? I'd hate it if someone had my name and did something like that. I mean, then everybody would be coming up to me and saying, 'Aren't you dead?' "

"That would be most disconcerting," the clerk agreed, "but just why do you need to know about your Suzanne Gray?"

"Okay, Jennifer," Leigh Ann said, giving her a little shove forward. "Go ahead and tell her."

Jennifer frowned. What the heck was Leigh Ann doing now?

"Tell her how . . ." Leigh Ann began, ". . . how Suzanne stole your entire wedding plans, how she swore she was going to wear exactly the same dress that you bought for your wedding for *her* wedding, the very week before yours. All the same guests are invited. We've already been to the florist and the bakery. She ordered the same flowers *and* the same wedding cake. Poor Jennifer had her heart set on a particular dress, this dress."

She grabbed the strapless size 2 off the rack.

"Yes. That is a lovely selection. It's close to two thousand dollars."

"Exactly. We need to know before we order it. With cash," Leigh Ann insisted. "And if you won't help us, we'll just have to take our business elsewhere. We've had to change all the other arrangements. If she's stolen the dress, too. . . ."

"Are you serious?" the woman asked.

Leigh Ann nodded her head vigorously. "It's pathetic really. You see they're marrying brothers. Only Jennifer got the good one — cute, thoughtful, successful. Suzanne wanted him, I mean she *really* wanted him. Only Jennifer came along and it was love at first sight. Just look at her. Who wouldn't fall in love with that sweet face?"

Leigh Ann nudged her and Jennifer tried to smile, despite the scowl between her eyes. Just wait until she had Leigh Ann alone. She was going to pay for this one.

"So Suzanne scooped up the other brother." Leigh Ann made a big dipping motion with her arms. "Jennifer set her wedding date, and then Suzanne set hers for one week before, in the same church. Suzanne has stolen every one of Jennifer's plans, right down to the blush of peach on the white roses she planned to carry, the caramel fudge wedding cake, and the little starbursts surrounding their names on the napkins. Jennifer and Oswald."

"Oswald?" Jennifer scowled anew.

"She calls him Ozzie. I forgot. Don't worry, Jen. That's what's printed on the napkins. I know because I ordered them.

The only thing poor Jennifer has left is the dress she's wanted to wear ever since she was a little girl, this Gawain original."

"This dress is new this year, part of his spring collection."

"Well, I know. It's as though this Gawain himself knew the time was right for Jennifer to get married and designed it just exactly like she'd always dreamed it. You can't let her be humiliated by purchasing the same gown as Suzanne. You just can't. You'd never get another wink of sleep. I know I wouldn't."

Leigh Ann gasped, let out a sob, and covered her face with a tissue. Jennifer saw one of Leigh Ann's eyes peep out to study the clerk. Good grief. She couldn't take Leigh Ann anywhere.

The clerk took a deep breath, and Jennifer prepared for a loud call for security. "If she bought that dress, I'll find it in our database. The nerve of some people. I've heard a lot of strange wedding stories, but this one is outrageous."

Jennifer couldn't agree more.

They followed the woman to the desk where she typed in Suzanne's name.

"Are you certain she shopped in this store?"

"That's where the swatches she had

came from," Jennifer assured her. "By the way, that's Gray with an *a.*"

"Okay. I've got it. A basic size twelve, completed last week and scheduled to be fitted yesterday."

"That means it was ready, that she could have picked it up," Jennifer said.

"Well, yes. Except for the alterations. But she seems to have missed her appointment." The clerk looked up and beamed. "Goodness. She ordered this dress back in November."

"You're kidding," Jennifer said, looking over the woman's shoulder at the screen. That was only about a month after Suzanne had first met Richard.

"These orders do take time. I'd suggest you get yours in immediately, certainly no later than next week, and even then we'll have to put a rush on it." She tapped a pencil impatiently against the monitor and then she smiled. "But you don't have to worry. This doesn't look at all like the dress you selected."

She turned the screen so Jennifer could see. There were two photos of the gown, one from the front and one from the back. It was lovely, with a lace overdress featuring a keyhole neckline. The strapless underdress was done in satin. The lace sleeves ended in a V over the back of each hand. The bodice was fitted, the skirt slightly gathered. Seed pearls and sequins were everywhere. The back view showed tiny covered buttons running from the neck all the way down the back to the start of an elegant train.

"I can pull up a photo of the veil she selected as well if you'd like," the clerk suggested.

Jennifer shook her head. She'd seen enough of Suzanne's shattered dreams.

"Ooooh. I want to see," Leigh Ann insisted.

"Tell me," the clerk went on, "who was that woman who was in here just before you, the one who was asking if anyone had been in to check on this Suzanne Gray woman's dress?"

Darn. It was too much to hope that the clerk had forgotten all about Belle.

"We haven't been totally honest with you," Leigh Ann began.

This was no time for a confessional.

"Actually there were three brothers, and —"

Jennifer grabbed Leigh Ann's arm before she could get out another word. "C'mon."

"But don't you want to place the order?" the clerk asked as Jennifer dragged Leigh

Ann toward the door.

"She'll be back," Leigh Ann promised. "I'll see to it." And with that Jennifer shoved her outside.

Chapter 23

"The deal was not that you go with me to the bridal boutique and then I go with you to the jewelers," Jennifer reminded Leigh Ann. "I was supposed to check on the dress; you were supposed to check on the ring."

"I know, I know, and I did but you've got to see this," Leigh Ann insisted, outside the door to Ziegler's Fine Jewelry. "You will not believe it."

"So you found the ring."

"I called around this morning, from work. Astor's didn't have a record of any jewelry purchase by either Richard Hovey or Suzanne Gray. So I phoned every other legitimate jeweler in Macon."

"And they told you right over the phone?"

"I said an order for a ring had been found among Hovey's belongings, and we were trying to determine if the ring had been received and the bill paid as part of settling his estate."

"How do you sleep at night?"

"I'm a storyteller. It's a God-given gift. Surely He expects me to use it. Besides, how else are you going to find out anything?"

"I thought you might just ask."

"Never work."

"And this did?"

"Like a charm. Richard Hovey purchased a three-carat diamond engagement ring, which he had sized and then picked up himself two months ago. The main stone is a marquise-cut, two-carat, colorless stone with a clarity of IF, surrounded by a cluster of smaller diamonds, all set in platinum."

"No one has found that ring," Jennifer pointed out.

"Exactly. Do you think it was stolen?"

"That's my guess. What else could have happened to it?"

Leigh Ann pulled Jennifer inside the small shop. The glass cases were laid out in a horseshoe with a repair and adjustment booth just past the farthest counter.

"I slipped over here during my break this morning. It's not exactly like it," Leigh Ann explained. "This one's not quite as expensive, but just look, third one in." She pointed at the back row of the second counter.

It glowed, catching every spark of light in the store and throwing it back with flashes of pink, yellow, and blue. Absolutely breathtaking.

"You'd have to love someone a whole lot to lay out that kind of money on a ring," Jennifer observed.

"Yeah. But isn't it spectacular? It's like one stone tosses the light to the next. Can you imagine the dance as you moved your hand back and forth?" Leigh Ann laid her hand on her shoulder, closed her eyes, and swayed. "Someday I want a ring just like that, don't you?"

"No. I'd be afraid to wear it out."

Leigh Ann's eyes popped open and she leaned forward for another look. "Maybe that's why no one ever saw Suzanne wearing it."

"I suspect you're right. That or maybe she — or he — wasn't quite ready to explain to everyone that they were getting married. He might have asked her to keep it quiet until he'd made things right with his family, broken the news to Ruth and his children. In the meantime she probably hid it in her drawer or more likely a safe deposit —"

"That one's quite wonderful. Would you like to see it?" The speaker must have been the store owner. He was a tall, slender, graying man dressed in a suit and wearing an unbelievably large, square-cut diamond set in a wide gold band on his right ring finger.

Leigh Ann's head bobbed up and down, but Jennifer said, "No, thank you. We're just looking."

Leigh Ann nudged her in the side. "We could just look up close."

"Aren't you late for work? It's almost two o' —"

"Oh my gosh! Can you drive me?" Leigh Ann pulled Jennifer out the door without so much as a thank you to the shop owner. "I won't have time to even park my car, let alone pick it up at the bridal boutique where we left it. If I'm really lucky I might just squeak in before my boss gets back."

Jennifer unlocked the doors to her car and Leigh Ann dove in, buckling her seat belt before Jennifer could get herself inside. She cranked the car and off they went with Leigh Ann leaning forward, tapping her fingers impatiently on the dash. They were less than a five-minute drive away. If the god of green lights was with them, they just might make it.

"Somebody's got that ring," Jennifer

said, just squeaking through a yellow light. "If Suzanne was wearing it when she died, and I would think she would have been, what happened to it?"

"You find that ring," Leigh Ann promised, "and you'll find Suzanne's murderer."

Chapter 24

"Okay, okay, Teague," Jennifer growled. "Would you please stop gloating long enough to answer my question?"

She'd much rather have put off the call to Teague until evening, but with Belle staying at her place, privacy was at a premium. And Belle had been out when Jennifer got back from dropping Leigh Ann at work.

"Hey, you called me, Marsh. Your little finger punched in my phone number, and you asked to speak to me. I knew you'd come crawling."

She hated that man, down to his scrawny little toes. How could someone so young — he couldn't possibly be more than twenty-five — have become so jaded?

Writing lies for a living for the *Atlanta Eye*. That's how.

"I have a hang-up device on this little phone of mine," she reminded him.

"Okay, Marsh. I'll stifle the gloat factor. So. What do you want to know about my esteemed colleague Belle Renard?"

"Belle decided to play detective. She apparently got in Simon DeSoto's good graces before he was brought up on charges, actually dated him for a while, maybe even —"

"Whoa, whoa, whoa. Who told you all this?" Teague asked.

"She did."

Jennifer could hear his cackle over the phone. "This is rich. That Belle. Always working every angle of every story. You know I'd really rather be telling you this in person. Over dinner perhaps. I could bring the beer. We could order in at your place. I'll be there as soon as I can get out of the office, say, about two hours."

"Teague, if you ever want me to speak to you again —"

"Speaking isn't all that essential."

Yuck. Why she ever talked to that man. "Tell me or —"

"Or what? Physical threats? What'd you have in mind? Rough's okay with me."

She paused, ready to slam the phone down with one more comment.

"You love him, don't you?" Teague asked. No sneering, nothing lewd about it. A statement of fact.

"I don't know," she said.

"Yes, you do. You know. You just haven't told yourself yet. And Belle Renard is not someone you want around him. She uses people, even people she cares about. I'm going to tell you this even though I probably shouldn't. And if she ever finds out I did, I probably won't survive the aftermath.

"She did correspond with DeSoto, but *after* he was convicted and sentenced to prison. *She* wrote *him,* hoping to get something in his handwriting, a confession she could use as the basis for a major story. She never lived with him in his apartment, if that's what you were about to say. Hell, she never even met him face-to-face, Marsh. And she never, in a million years, thought he'd get that conviction overturned."

"So she really is frightened?"

"Hell, I don't know. But if you wrote the kind of stuff I suspect she put in those letters to a man who killed his wife, you'd be more than a little unsettled when he got loose, too. That Belle — she's got one hell of an imagination."

Terrific.

"I don't suppose you were in the office when DeSoto showed up Tuesday morning?"

"Lucked out with that one. Watched the man make one spectacular fool of himself, wanting to know where Belle was. Even got a photo that will be out in today's paper. Unfortunately he declined an interview, and the big honcho here nixed the story I wrote to go with it. He found it inflammatory."

"Yeah, right. Scared of a lawsuit, huh?"

"Absolutely and he doesn't scare easily. DeSoto has the best of the best defending him.

"By the way, I knew it was bogus," Teague added.

"What?"

"The engagement announcement. Belle told everyone in the office about it the Friday before it came out. I knew it wasn't true, that she'd had it put in the newspaper without his permission."

"How did you know that?"

"Because if I know anything, I know that Sam Culpepper is in love with you."

And for some reason when this pariah of human life said those words, they really seemed true. God. What was she going to do?

"But, hey, that doesn't mean you and I can't have wild sex. I wasn't exactly looking for a lifetime commitment, you know. You get bored with Sam, and all you have to do is whistle."

"Thanks, Teague."

"You don't have to thank me. Teague's twenty-four-hour love service is at your command."

"Right." So much for a tender moment.

"Like I said, watch Belle. She plays every angle."

"Was she ever involved with anyone that you know of?"

"You mean seriously? That I wouldn't know, but I do know it'd take one hell of a man to rein her in."

"Do you think DeSoto will do her harm if he finds her?"

"Don't ask me to guess, Marsh. Anger is one of those things. I don't know the man, and he really wanted to talk to her."

It made her shudder to think about it, even though Belle had created her own mess.

"One more thing," Jennifer said. She wasn't likely to call him back. "Your paper printed a story about Suzanne Gray and Lewis Spikes."

"Yeah, that gal that froze herself solid. Great copy. The Spikes story, one of the other guys dug that one up. The editor made him soft-pedal that one, too. Felt too much sympathy for the deceased might make for a backlash, but she was pursuing this guy in high school like nobody's business. He had to take a restraining order out against her. She was so in loooooove with the dude that she wouldn't leave him alone. Embarrassing for all parties involved. Something for you to remember Marsh. A woman throws herself at a man, some get a restraining order. Others are more than happy to give in. Like I said, you watch Belle around your man. She still staying with him?"

"Nope. She's staying with me."

Teague let out a belly laugh. "Marsh, you've got to be kidding me. That's your biggest flaw. You don't know how to blow people off."

Oh, yes she did. "Thanks, Teague. Later." And with that she hung up the phone.

Chapter 25

"Okay, let's lay it all out." Monique handed out small pads of paper. First to April parked in her customary spot on the sofa, next to Leigh Ann buried in the pillows of the corner sectional, then to Jennifer sitting next to her, and lastly to Teri, sitting cross-legged on the floor.

"What's this for?" April asked.

"To take notes," Monique explained. "Jennifer is the only true mystery writer in the group. I thought it might help the rest of us to keep up with what was going on."

"You mean like in the game Clue," Leigh Ann suggested, tucking her legs up under her, "where you write down where Miss Scarlet was when and what happened to the rope and the candlestick."

"Exactly like that." Monique's voice could not have been more sarcastic.

"So, Teri, you had the florist."

Teri pulled a card out of her pocket. "Twenty-four centerpieces, all in fresh-cut flowers in hues of dark purple to the palest pink, with huge white mums sprinkled throughout. Three giant arrangements of gladiolas and mixed flowers for the altar, another for the main reception table. The bride's bouquet was to be white roses accented in the palest pink and the boutonnieres were to be in the dark purple to maroon range. You don't even want to know what it was going to cost."

"Was the final order ever put in?"

Teri shook her head. "No date was set. No deposit was made, only the estimates. Suzanne was in there making the arrangements last month."

"April," Monique said.

"Do you know they have actual samples of every cake they make at Lazy Susan's? I wish I'd skipped lunch. The kids had a ball."

"You took them with you?" Teri asked.

"I couldn't very well leave them at home, and I can't afford to get a babysitter just to run down to the bakery. Besides, they loved it. The lemonade cake was Jonathan's favorite. Colleen liked the chocolate dream cake best."

"Of course she would. Chocolate is essential to every woman's diet, even when she's only a year old," Leigh Ann said.

"So what was the final order?" Jennifer asked.

"A strawberry chiffon with cream-cheese icing in four tiers. Enough to serve three hundred guests plus two backup sheet cakes in the same flavor. Personally I would have gone with the peach delight. It had a much better flavor, but I suspect Suzanne wanted the pink. And she selected a groom's cake of mint chocolate with fudge icing. Mint. Not everybody likes it, you know."

"Deposits?" Monique asked.

"No. Not until the date was set. Sometime in June. She was to come back early this week to make the final arrangements."

Monique nodded. "Same thing at the stationers. Five hundred invitations. Colorful, floral on heavy white stock with script lettering. No final order. No deposit."

"I did check at Talley's Travels," Monique added. "Suzanne had been in, but she didn't book anything. On an off chance, I asked my own travel agent to see if she could find out if Richard Hovey had."

"And . . ." Jennifer sat up.

"A cruise for two to the Bahamas, slated for August."

"Really," Jennifer said. "But not through Talley's."

"No," Monique assured her.

That would have been about the time the newspaper article implied that Ruth and Richard would be getting remarried.

"Did he give a name for his traveling companion?"

"Yes. Mrs. Richard Hovey."

Jennifer looked around the room, from one face to another, as though she was beginning to see the picture for the first time. "You all *do* see what's missing here. Did Richard Hovey show up at any of the places you visited?"

The group gave a collective shake of their heads.

"Not once? Other than the travel arrangements and the ring, had any of the people you spoke with actually had a conversation with Hovey?"

Again the shake.

They all looked at each other. "Are you thinking what I'm thinking?" Jennifer asked.

"Saying something doesn't make it so," April declared. "Was Suzanne Gray really marrying Richard Hovey or —"

"Just a minute! I'm not sure what you're implying," Leigh Ann said, "but a woman killed herself —"

"Over a man who may not have even known she was alive," Jennifer finished.

Chapter 26

As soon as Jennifer got home, she swept past Belle, who was sitting on the sofa eating popcorn and watching TV, and grabbed the phone book from under the end table. Muffy, not about to miss out on any possible excitement, followed her straight to her bedroom where she closed the door. She had one more lead to check before she wrote off Suzanne Gray as Richard Hovey's Juliet.

Lewis Spikes. Some trouble back in high school with Suzanne. If there was a juvenile record, it'd be sealed, and she knew better than to trust the *Atlanta Eye*'s account. But sealed or not, Mr. Spikes, assuming she could find him, was under no obligation to keep what he knew to himself.

She dumped her purse on the bed and flipped through the telephone book to S. One thing about Macon, a lot of folks who were born and brought up there continued to make it their home. Her finger ran down the page. Spainhour. Spencer. Spikes, Jeffrey; Spikes, L. B.; Spikes, Lewis.

Jennifer punched the number into the phone.

"Hello." A woman's voice. Darn it all.

"Mrs. Spikes?"

"Yes."

"This is Jennifer Marsh. I'm trying to contact a Lewis Spikes who attended Sherwood High School about twenty years ago."

"Could you tell me what this is in reference to?"

"Of course, but I'd prefer to speak to Mr. Spikes."

"He's not home. Were you one of our classmates?" the woman asked.

Our. "No, but maybe you can help me after all. Did you know a Suzanne Gray?"

Jennifer could hear the woman's breathing right across the line.

"What of it? She's dead."

"Can you tell me about her relationship with your husband? Mrs. Spikes, it's really important." Jennifer took a deep breath. "Did Suzanne ever claim —"

"It was all lies. Every bit of it. She had the whole school believing they were dating when she was chasing him night and day. There's no other word for it. She made our lives a living hell. And that's all I intend to say about it. Don't call here again."

The phone buzzed in her ear.

Lewis Spikes twenty years ago. Richard Hovey this year. Had there been others in between? What was Richard's relationship to Suzanne really like?

She hung up the phone and then scooped it right back up, punching in Sam's phone number. He sounded groggy, as though she'd caught him in the middle of a nap. "I think Richard Hovey and Suzanne Gray were never involved. Heck, I'm not even sure he knew her."

"Jennifer . . ."

"Listen to me, Sam. Suzanne flat-out stalked some guy in high school. All those wedding preparations, all that talk, she —"

"Her fingerprints were in his bedroom. And his bathroom. His kitchen."

"Oh." Jennifer slumped back on the bed. Another theory down the tubes. "When did you find that out?"

"Late this afternoon. I asked them to run a check."

Sam had friends in the police department. He'd helped them more than once, and they'd learned to listen to him.

"They took fingerprints from the scene before Hovey's death was ruled an accident," Sam assured her. "It's routine. I knew they'd have Suzanne's from the autopsy. And I knew you'd eventually be calling, asking me just that. Suzanne was in his house, many times from the look of it. Whether they were actually engaged or not, I couldn't tell you."

She let out a loud breath. "He didn't show up anywhere to help her select wedding arrangements."

"So?"

Men. Even Sam, who was so with it, could understand a man's willingness to sit back and let someone else make all the decisions about his wedding day.

"Never mind. I'm sorry I bothered you. It's just that . . ."

"What?" Sam asked.

"It's just that the more I learn about Suzanne, the more I can't see her with Richard Hovey."

There was a pause on the other end of the line. "Let me tell you about a secret only we men know," Sam said. "When we fall in love, we fall hard. A lot of us don't ever fall completely out, no matter what happens in the meantime. And we fall for a certain type of woman. If he once loved Ruth, he might have loved Suzanne, don't you think?"

"The only characteristics Ruth Hovey shared with Suzanne Gray were age, hair color, and a similar body type. I suspect personality-wise they were entirely different people. And there's one more flaw to your theory: Richard had to have once loved Ruth, not just her money, loved her so much he wanted to re-create that love."

"I'd like to think he did."

Sam, the romantic.

"I'd like to think so, too. But Richard Hovey could have had half the female population of Macon. He was an edgy kind of guy. I'd think he'd want someone more exciting, someone who would offer him a challenge. And, Sam, Suzanne exhibited stalker behavior at least one time in the past with a boy in high school. Even Marjorie implied something had gone on with Vic. I just don't see it. I don't think Hovey would have given her a first look, let alone a second, not with Ruth herself waiting in the wings."

"Okay, but then why did she die?"

Jennifer sighed. Why did he have to be so darned logical? "I have no idea. Talk to you tomorrow?"

"Of course."

She hung up the phone. Maybe Suzanne's behavior in high school had only been an overzealous first love. It happens.

And maybe none of this made any sense.

She picked up the phone again and punched in the number to the Starvin' Marvin. A quiet little voice answered.

"Suzie?"

"Jennifer?"

"Yeah. Listen. You know you told me your aunt had a big box of photos of her past boyfriends. Is there any way you could get hold of it, and we could look through them together?"

"Sure. All I have to do is go down to her house. I know exactly where it is."

"Great. Are you free in the morning? Say about ten?"

"That would be good. You want to meet me there? At her house?"

"I'll be there." Jennifer dropped the receiver back into the cradle. Maybe in that stack of photos was a man who didn't like his picture taken. Or one who had had it with too much uninvited attention.

Belle would be needing the bedroom and she'd be needing her computer. It was past ten o'clock, but she'd been putting off something she had to do.

"You can have the room back now," Jennifer announced from the doorway.

Belle didn't move from the sofa. She just continued to munch her popcorn.

"Look. It's been a long day, and I need to get to sleep. Do you mind? There's another TV in the bedroom."

Belle rolled her eyes and used the remote to flip off the TV. She set the bucket of popcorn down on the end table and brushed the salt off her hands. "Okay, sure." Then popped one last kernel into her mouth.

Jennifer pulled the sheets and blanket off the chair and spread them over the couch, but as soon as Belle was out of the room, Muffy trailing after her, she went to her computer, turned it on, and slipped the disk Sam had given her out of her pocket and into the drive.

Thank God, he'd transcribed those tapes. But how was she ever going to get through it all? There were pages and pages. Only one way: sit down and read the whole thing.

She must have dozed off, because she didn't hear Belle until she was standing right over her shoulder.

"What's that? Sam's files?"

Jennifer nodded, rubbing her eyes. No use denying it, the woman could read what was on the screen.

"Finding anything interesting?"

Jennifer yawned and stretched. "Not particularly. What are you doing up?"

"I got hungry. Want to split a peanut butter and jelly sandwich?"

"Sure. You making?"

"It's one of my specialties. The secret is extra jelly. You do have grape."

"Can't make peanut butter and jelly without it," Jennifer agreed. "I'll pour us some milk." She followed Belle into the kitchen.

"You've only got smooth. Chunky's the best. So what do you think?" Belle asked, pulling the peanut butter out of the cupboard.

"Go ahead and make two sandwiches. One's not going to be enough."

"No, I mean about Suzanne."

"I think she wasn't the woman Hovey bought a three-carat diamond ring for."

Belle let the knife drop back into the jar and leaned against the counter. "Geez. That must have cost him a fortune. So what's your theory?"

"I think there was another woman."

Belle nodded. "That's what I was thinking, too. Ruth, maybe?"

"Maybe. Or Kelli Byers."

Belle snorted. "That screwball?"

"Hey, she was leaving roses on the man's grave."

"Really? What'd you do? Catch her in the act?"

"Something like that."

"Jennifer, you are something else." Belle shook her head. "What'd you find in Sam's interviews with Hovey? Any mention of another woman?"

"Yeah. Indirectly. I'm not surprised Sam didn't catch it. He probably never would. When Hovey talked about traveling or retirement, he used the word *we* consistently, and it wasn't the royal we. He didn't use it anywhere else. Too much of an egomaniac, I'm sure."

"He still could have meant Suzanne, if that's all he said."

Jennifer yawned and shook her head. "He was referring to a trip to Puerto Rico that happened about eighteen months ago and another to the Virgin Islands sometime in September. He didn't meet Suzanne until after that."

Jennifer took the sandwich Belle handed her. "I can barely keep my eyes open."

"I'm not surprised. It's after one."

"Cripes. Not again."

Jennifer took a bite of sandwich. "Hey, this is good."

"Yeah. It's easy to forget how really good they are." Belle paused. "Jennifer, I'm sorry."

Jennifer stared at her. So what was the catch? "About what?"

"Causing trouble between you and Sam. I know I can be thoughtless, and sometimes people who don't know me might think I'm callous or insensitive."

And people who did know her.

"I really would like to help you and Sam with the story. No strings attached. No stealing bylines, I promise. It'll help keep my mind occupied, keep me from thinking about DeSoto." For a moment Belle looked genuinely afraid, vulnerable. "You and Sam have something special."

"You ever been in love?" Jennifer asked.

"You mean the real thing?"

"Not the imitation variety."

Belle smiled. "Hasn't everyone?"

"Who was he?"

"A photojournalist. I met him when I was working in Philly. He went on assignment in Central America and he never came back."

"I'm sorry."

Belle smiled again, a normal smile this time, nothing little-girl or pretentious about it. "Tell you what, you've been so nice to let me stay with you, what if I take you out to lunch tomorrow? For something better than peanut butter and jelly."

"Sounds good," Jennifer agreed.

"Terrific."

Chapter 27

Jennifer couldn't help but steal a look over her shoulder as she knocked on Suzanne's door. She could almost feel Kelli Byers watching from her window across the street. The woman needed to get a real job, or at least a life.

Suzanne's little house looked deserted. No lights, at least that she could see, were on inside. No car in the drive except her own. Where was Suzie? She turned to look up the road toward Marjorie's when the door came open behind her, making her jump.

"How'd you get here?" she asked Suzie.

"I jogged down from the house. It's not that far. Come on in. I've got the box."

Spread out on the braided area rug in front of the sofa was a boot-sized shoe box with the lid off. Suzie scooted down on the floor and Jennifer joined her. The box was brimming with photos, all of men.

"Do you know who any of these people are?" Jennifer asked, turning over the ones on top. None of them were labeled.

"I don't remember their names. When I was little, Aunt Suzanne used to get them down and go through them with me, but I've forgotten, except for the one of our minister. That one's supposed to be a secret. Nothing really happened between them, but he was crazy about her. She didn't want his wife to find out and she certainly didn't want the congregation to know.

"I used to come up here and spend the night with Aunt Suzanne and she'd tell me the story behind each one. She'd meet them dancing or at the bars — Mama wasn't supposed to know Aunt Suzanne went out drinking — or the bowling alley. All kinds of places. Even the grocery store."

Jennifer's face must have shown the skepticism she felt because Suzie said, "Oh, I know what you're thinking. You wonder how a woman like Aunt Suzanne could attract so many men. She and I look an awful lot alike and I've only had one boyfriend my whole life. But I figure it's the difference between the two of us. You see, she had this confidence about her. She didn't let anything stand in the way of something she wanted. Not anything.

That's attractive, don't you think? That determination."

Could be. And then there was Belle.

"Why didn't she marry one of these guys?" Jennifer asked.

"It just never worked out, I guess. And she was waiting for that special one to come along. Waiting for her Richard."

"I don't suppose you'd know it if she parted on bad terms with any of them?"

"Aunt Suzanne? I can't imagine that."

Asking a niece to speak ill of her favorite aunt — okay, only aunt — probably wasn't going to get a realistic answer.

Jennifer noticed one photo lying by itself on the sofa cushion. She picked it up. It looked to be several years old. It was of a man leaning back against the grill of a pickup, wearing jeans, a western shirt, a belt with a huge buckle, and cowboy boots. He was grinning for the camera.

"Why'd you pull this one out?"

"Oh, that's my dad. Doesn't he look spiffy?"

"Vic Turner?"

"Yeah. I don't know how it got in here. By accident, I guess."

Right. By accident.

Jennifer sifted down through the box. A few of the photos were studio shots. How she got those, one could only guess. But most of them were snapshots, several of each man. "Did your aunt have a camera?" Jennifer asked.

"Of course."

"Do you know where it is?"

Suzie hopped up and dug in the top of the coat closet. She pulled out a camera bag, toted it back to the rug, and set it down for Jennifer to examine. It was a Nikon 35mm. And tucked in one of the side pockets of the bag was a telephoto lens.

"Did you ever see any of these men come to your aunt's house, ever meet any of them?"

"Aunt Suzanne said my dad wouldn't approve. He was pretty protective of her, a single woman living alone like she did. He had to kind of watch out after her. She told me she had to meet them somewhere, so he wouldn't get upset, and then they'd go off on their dates. She made me promise not to mention anything about them to Mom or Dad. I don't think she liked Kelli getting all into her business either."

That was probably true.

Suzie grabbed up a handful of photos and held them against her chest. "Can you imagine having all these men in love with you?"

Jennifer shook her head. She couldn't imagine all of them being in love with Suzanne Gray either. And Suzie was holding proof of that right in her hand. Not a single one of those photos included Suzanne Gray.

Chapter 28

"I was beginning to think you weren't going to show," Belle called out from the couch as Jennifer burst through the door of her apartment and dumped her purse on a dining chair. "Where were you all morning?"

Muffy scrambled off the sofa and slunk behind Belle's feet.

"I saw that," Jennifer warned.

"Oops. Sorry we forgot," Belle said.

"Right. I'm sure you did."

"You ready to go?"

"Oh, lunch. That's right." Jennifer checked her watch. "What'd you have in mind?"

"There's a new seafood —"

"I don't do seafood, nothing with a face."

"Do shrimp have faces?"

"With eyes, mouths, and feelers and lots of yucky legs."

"Oysters don't. Do they?"

"No and neither do anemones. I don't eat them either."

"Okay. Then let's skip the ocean life. How about Applebee's on Tom Hill?"

"Sure, fine, whatever." She grabbed the phone off the wall between the kitchen and the dining area and punched in Sam's number. All she got was his voice mail. She hung up without leaving a message. "Double darn." She didn't want to page him in case he was in court.

"Hey, relax," Belle told her. "You've been running around day and night with this Gray-Hovey thing. You need some quiet time. I'll call and make a reservation. How long do you need before you'll be ready to go?"

"Give me ten minutes. Fifteen at the most. But I really don't think they accept reservations."

Jennifer took off for the bedroom and shut the door. She needed time alone to regroup. She sat down on the edge of the bed that Belle hadn't bothered to make, closed her eyes, and took her head in her hands.

Suzanne was stalking Richard Hovey. She was as certain of it as she'd ever been of anything. Suzanne's impending birthday and his notoriety must have pushed her over the edge, exploding her latest infatuation into a 3-D fantasy complete with storybook wedding.

Of course Hovey's family didn't know about the wedding. No one did except for the people Suzanne told — her family and her friends — because it only existed in Suzanne's mind.

Hovey knew, though, at least that she was interested in him. He'd had to deal with it. Quietly. The phone calls Suzanne had made to his office. He'd tried to put her off, but it hadn't worked.

So if he never was in love with Suzanne, who, blast it, was Hovey waiting for the night he slipped and died? Did it matter?

It wasn't Ruth, or she wouldn't have been so quick to buy Jennifer off. Who did that leave? Kelli Byers? Would Hovey have given her a toss in the sheets? Probably. She was attractive and what had Ruth called her husband? A bottom feeder? But would he have sprung for a bottle of Silver Oak, spread rose petals, and lighted candles for her? Highly unlikely. Most men wouldn't do that for the loves of their lives. Most men . . .

Most men wouldn't do it at all.

Rose petals, candles, a warm bath with scented oils — that was a woman's fantasy, not a man's. They'd been looking at this all wrong.

Of course. It had been staring them all right in the face all the time.

What if a woman had set up that seduction scene the night Hovey had died? It had to be someone who had a key to Hovey's house. Someone who knew his favorite kind of wine. It had to be . . .

Suzanne Gray. Because if she had, it might just explain why she had been murdered.

But something went terribly wrong. Hovey had died. Why? Because he climbed the stairs and found rose petals and a strange woman in his house? What did he do? Tell her to get out? Laugh at her? Explain that he was in love with someone else? Had she pushed him? Or had he slipped? Did she mean to kill him?

Either way, he went down those stairs and died at the bottom.

Her mind rushed on. But how did Suzanne get a key to let herself in? She'd been there all right. Sam said her fingerprints were all over Hovey's house.

Even as Jennifer posed the question, the answer slipped right into her mind. The balloon delivery. The one Ruth had hired her to make. Marjorie said Ruth had given Suzanne a key to fill the house with balloons, set up his favorite wine, and set the scene. She could have had the key copied, and that explained how she knew Hovey's favorite wine.

Jennifer felt sweat bead across her forehead, but not from any heat. The relentless cold spell that had gripped Macon had finally broken that morning, but it was still winter outside.

Suzanne had been murdered. Any doubt Jennifer had ever had otherwise was completely gone. Because with Hovey dead, what was there to keep her from moving on to the next great love of her life? Wasn't that what she'd always done before? All she had to do was insert a different name in all her wedding plans. She'd already demonstrated she didn't need the man's consent.

But even if this time was somehow different and Suzanne was in utter despair over Hovey's death, even if she had decided to kill herself over this man who had never been a part of her life except for a balloon delivery, she would have done it up right. She was already in high fantasy mode. The wedding dress she'd ordered was ready. She could have picked it up, had it fitted early, or not bothered. And the roses Jennifer had dug out of Marjorie's trash can came complete with thorns. Why not order the bridal bouquet she'd selected? Suzanne had charge cards, if money was an issue. She obviously didn't plan to be around later to worry about any of the bills.

So murder it was. Jennifer was as certain about this as she'd been about anything in her life.

"You all right in there?" Belle called.

"Peachy keen." Why didn't that woman just go away? One "I'm sorry" and a single heart-to-heart over peanut butter and jelly did not a friend make. She made a mental note to call around to the motels and hotels again when they got back. Surely out of all those Jehovah's Witnesses, one had been called away on emergency. There had to be someplace else Belle could stay.

"I'm getting hungry out here," Belle called again.

"All right, all right. I'm going to try Sam one more time before we go."

But, again, Sam failed to answer.

She gave herself a quick once-over in the mirror, not that she particularly cared how she looked. She wasn't out to impress Belle. How long could lunch take anyway? And they both had to eat. She took a deep breath and went into the living room.

She found Belle next to the refrigerator talking baby talk to Muffy and feeding her a whole handful of treats.

"Hey, go easy," Jennifer told her. "A fat dog is not a healthy dog. You sure it's all right for you to go out? DeSoto may still be around."

"I'm getting claustrophobic. You can't expect me to stay in all day, every day. Besides, he has no idea where I am."

Belle grabbed her purse and Muffy scampered, whimpering after her. After *her.* First she tries to take her man and now she was working on her dog.

Jennifer grabbed Muffy around the collar and kissed at her. "You be good while we're gone." Then she shoved the dog back inside and shut the door.

Chapter 29

Jennifer and Belle took the stairs and were on the front steps in less than two minutes.

"I'll drive," Belle offered. "I'm at the far end of the lot, near the pines." Jennifer could see the car. Belle had backed into the very last space.

"Where'd you go this morning?" Belle asked. "I've hardly seen you since I moved in."

"I've had things I had to do."

"For Sam? Did you finally get him on the phone?"

Jennifer shook her head.

"You seem awfully anxious to talk to him."

Jennifer stopped dead on the sidewalk. "If you're going to spend lunch grilling me about Sam —"

"No. I'm sorry. I've been cooped up and Jerry Springer doesn't provide a lot of topics for conversation. Tell me, when did you become a vegetarian?"

Jennifer threw her a sidelong look, and

they started on down the walk. "It was one of those college revelations. We were studying animal communication in psychology and I suddenly realized they have sophisticated societal structures. I just couldn't do it anymore. Even ants communicate back and forth, fight wars, keep aphids for 'milk,' raise crops. Disturb their nests, and they hightail it out of there with their babies. They live in such a dangerous world. It's fascinating."

"Sounds like it."

Jennifer headed around to the passenger side of the Miata. The hardtop was on for the winter. She tugged on the door handle, but it was locked. The movement made her shoulder bag slide down to her wrist and bump against the door, spilling her sunglasses and keys out onto the pavement.

"Cripes. Belle, can you get this car open? That button you pushed didn't do a thing." She ducked to pick up her things.

It sounded like a backfire behind her followed by glass shattering in front of her. She rose up to see the entire front passenger window on the maroon minivan in the next space missing. And Belle gone. In one surreal moment, she turned in the direction of the noise and realized it had come from the wooded area behind her, not from the road. She dove to the pavement just as another boom sounded and more glass splintered.

"Belle! Belle! Where are you?"

"I'm here." Belle's voice sounded muffled. It was coming from the other side of the car. "Are you all right?"

"I think so. Are you?"

Jennifer was flat against the pavement but still exposed and shaking hard. Nothing stood between her and that stand of trees. She forced herself forward, half rolling, half crawling around to the front bumper. "Stay down. I think it's a rifle."

"How do you know that?"

"From the way that window broke. And the distance. I don't think anyone would try using a pistol for a shot like that. No telling how many shots he has left."

Peeking under the car, she could see Belle's legs where she was crouching between the Miata and the minivan. She drew her legs up under her and, keeping her head low, scooted to Belle, glass crunching under her shoes. At least they were shielded. Their only hope was for the assailant not to come out of the woods, not to risk exposing himself to the road and passersby. If he did, they'd both be dead before they could stand up.

Glass was sprinkled all over Belle's beautiful curly hair and the shoulders of her coat. She appeared to be in shock, her eyes huge, angry.

Jennifer grabbed Belle's hand and pulled her forward. "Come on. We need to get out of here before he comes checking to see if he got you."

Using the cars as cover, they managed to make it back to the entrance of the building. They made a dash to the front steps, scurried inside, and then flew up the stairs. At her door, Jennifer fumbled with her keys, looking over her shoulder, half expecting to see Simon DeSoto swagger out of the stairwell at any moment with a gun pointed straight at their heads.

Somehow she got the right key into the lock and turned it. Muffy woofed and danced around them as Jennifer pulled Belle inside, pushed the door shut, and threw the massive lock on her door. She'd had one break-in and had vowed never to have another. Nothing short of a stick of dynamite would be getting past that lock.

Her legs gave way and she slid to the floor. Muffy was all over her licking her face and whining. That's when she looked down and saw the huge tear in her pants leg and blood all over it. "Damn it! These are my favorite pants."

Belle eased to the floor next to her. Her hands were shaking and one was streaked red. She was mumbling something that Jennifer couldn't make out except for a four-letter word here and there.

She put an arm around Belle and pulled her into a hug. "We've got to call the police," she choked. "Call the police and tell them Simon DeSoto just tried to kill you."

Chapter 30

"No, I can't give you a description of him or his clothes. I didn't see his face. I didn't see him. I don't even know for sure it was a man," Jennifer told the young female police officer sitting across the dining table from her. "I didn't see anything except glass flying."

She took a sip of hot tea. It helped to have something warm and comforting to hold on to, and the more she drank of it, the more she suspected there was more than tea in that pot. Maybe a hint of bourbon?

Mrs. Ramon had prepared it and brought it over for her and Belle. She, too, had heard the shots, but she wasn't sure what she should do. The police gave her an err-on-the-side-of-caution lecture and let her go home. But before she went, she'd leaned down to Jennifer and whispered, nodding in Belle's direction, "So, better here with you than with your man."

Somehow who was with whom paled in

the assurance that they were both safe.

"Why are you so sure it was a rifle?" the young officer asked, looking up from her notes. Jennifer noticed how pretty she was. Blonde with lots of bangs and a French braid. She wondered if she'd ever been shot at.

"It just sounded like it. I didn't see any pellet marks, so it wasn't a shotgun. And it was accurate. He had to be, what, sixty feet or more from us?"

"He wasn't accurate enough to hit you."

"We were moving. If my purse hadn't slipped off my shoulder and if Belle hadn't . . . Is Belle all right?"

"Ms. Renard is fine. Just a little shook up. She's in the bedroom, speaking with another officer."

They didn't want them to contaminate each other's accounts.

"You should look through the woods," Jennifer suggested. "If he didn't pick them up, there may be shell casings out there."

"Someone's taking care of that."

The door was ajar, what with all the officers coming in and out. Poor Muffy had been relegated to the bathroom, and she wasn't at all pleased about it. Jennifer could hear her scratching at the door and then jumping in and out of the bathtub, ringing it like a low-pitched bell. Poor thing. That trick usually got her let out.

It took her a moment before she realized it was Sam's voice she heard in the outside hallway, speaking her name. And then another voice said something about "no press."

She was on her none-too-steady feet, calling for him.

He pushed past the officer at the door, and when she saw him, she lost it, dissolving into tears.

"Hey, hey," he said, taking her into his arms. "It's all right."

"There were bullets and flying glass and Belle. . . ." she snuffled against his shoulder. "I didn't know what to do."

He shushed her. "It's okay. You did good. They told me you got yourself and Belle out of there. That's all you needed to do." He pulled back and looked her over. He frowned at the bandage running from her knee to her ankle. "You're hurt."

"The paramedics checked her out," the officer assured him. "She's suffered some abrasions from contact with the asphalt, but she should be just fine. Miss Marsh refused transport to the hospital."

"If anything happened to you —"

"Not me, Sam. It had to have been

DeSoto. He really is trying to kill Belle."

She could see him pale. "How is she?"

"All right, I think. They picked a lot of glass out of her hair, but except for a few scratches and one fairly deep cut on her hand, I think she's okay. She was lucky she had on a fairly heavy coat."

"Did you tell them about DeSoto?"

Jennifer shook her head. "I'm letting Belle do that. I'd just be repeating what she told us and I didn't want to get any of it wrong. Besides, neither one of us actually saw anything."

He hugged her tight. It made her bite her tongue. She had one heck of a bruise on her right shoulder where she hit the ground. Sam loosened his grip and eased her back onto the dining chair.

"Are you finished?" he asked the officer.

"If I wasn't, I would have thrown you out." She closed her notebook. "You might want to see about getting her something to eat."

"My stomach's been growling," Jennifer admitted. "Hideous, horrible, loud rumbling sounds. Unbelievably embarrassing." It was almost three o'clock and all she'd had to eat all day was one slice of toast.

"Why didn't you call me?"

"They asked me to wait. How did you find out?"

"Mrs. Ramon. She paged me. I was in court."

Jennifer smiled and took another sip of tea. A little more of Mrs. Ramon's home brew and she wouldn't care if she ate or not, especially now that Sam was here.

She looked up over the cup rim to see a tall officer coming out of the bedroom. He addressed the woman who'd been interviewing Jennifer. "I want you to take Ms. Renard to the emergency room while I write up this report."

"The emergency room?" Jennifer started to rise in her seat.

"No, it's okay," Belle said, coming up behind him. "The bleeding stopped, but the wound's still gaping." She had a bandage wrapped around her left hand.

Jennifer nodded. "You don't want it to scar."

When she saw Sam, Belle put her hand to her mouth as though holding back tears. He went to her and hugged her, too. "Have them bring you back here," he told her.

She nodded, clinging to him.

"I'm going to walk her out," Sam said.

The officer got up and thanked Jennifer, and the three of them left.

She let out a sigh of relief. Quiet had never felt so good. Her head was pounding right along with her heart, which was just now beginning to slow down. She lay down on the couch and closed her eyes, promising herself five minutes to regroup. Muffy had calmed down some in the bathroom now that everyone was gone. As soon as Sam got back, she'd let her out and lock the front door. Then she'd tell him what she'd figured out about the night Hovey died. And then find them all something to eat. Then go to sleep. No. Sleep, then eat. No. . . .

"Jennifer."

Her eyes drifted open. Sam was staring down at her, upside down. She must have her head in his lap. His sleeves were rolled to the elbows and his tie was loose. He looked really good. Except for the sour expression on his face.

Hmmmmmm, Sam. It's nice that he's here. Her eyes drifted shut again.

"Jennifer, wake up."

"Why? I'm not asleep. I just lay down to rest my eyes." She pushed herself up on her elbows. It'd gotten dark outside and Sam had forgotten to shut the blinds. Wasn't that just like a man? But it wasn't as though they were on the first floor. She shook herself awake. Muffy rose up from her spot next to the sofa and licked her hand.

"Listen. Belle, get yourself in here."

Belle came around the partition to the kitchen, a Chinese take-out carton in her hand. "I was just putting the lo mein into a bowl."

"That can wait." Sam used the remote control to turn up the sound on the television just as a voice said, "Welcome to the Six O'clock News. The body of Simon DeSoto has been found shot to death in an alley not far from the offices of Hovey, Trainer, and Palmer. More than a year ago Mr. DeSoto had been convicted of the murder of his wife, Nadine DeSoto, but that conviction was recently overturned. DeSoto is reported to have left the law offices of his attorney, Alvin Trainer, partner of the deceased Richard Hovey, this afternoon at approximately four o'clock P.M., after a meeting with Mr. Trainer that lasted an estimated hour and a half. Again, alleged wife-murderer Simon DeSoto has been found shot to death. We'll bring you further details as they become available to us."

Jennifer sat all the way up, threw her legs to the floor, and winced. She was as awake as she'd ever been in her life.

"Sam. The restraining order. What if the police think you're the one —"

"They won't. I can account for my time."

Jennifer turned to stare at Belle. "You're home. And safe. Did you hear that?"

Belle nodded, dropping down on the sofa arm next to Sam.

"But your hand . . . Are you all right?" Jennifer asked. For a moment she felt disoriented, as though she'd dreamed being out in the parking lot, bullets whizzing past.

Belle touched the gauze that covered her hand and her wrist. "Fine. They put in a couple of stitches and sent me home."

"Hey, hey. Calm down," Sam soothed, putting an arm around Jennifer. "Belle got back maybe thirty minutes ago. She took a cab from the hospital."

"Thank God. Is he really dead, Sam?"

"So it seems."

"Then it's over."

But her relief lasted only a few seconds. She took in Sam's dark expression. And Belle's as she studied Sam's face.

And then it hit her, too.

"Why is DeSoto dead? Sam, who killed him?"

Chapter 31

Sam fed them the Chinese takeout, put Jennifer to bed on the couch, and went home, after she insisted that he do just that. She'd talk to him in the morning, tell him what she knew then, when her head was clearer.

But she couldn't sleep. She tossed and turned, pounding the pillows, trying to find some outlet for her exhaustion.

The sound of Belle's snoring drifted into the living room. Not a loud, in-your-face-keep-you-awake snore, more like a dainty I'm-not-perfect little snore.

But it wasn't Belle that was keeping her awake, or even the light from the kitchen. It was the whys shouting at her from the dark. Why had Suzanne been murdered? If her theory was right, that Suzanne had killed Hovey by accident or design, who had found out about it and how? And why had DeSoto been killed? Did the one have anything to do with the other?

They both knew Richard Hovey. Both of

their futures depended on him, DeSoto's in the real world, Suzanne's in some fantasy creation. But Hovey was dead before either of them. Had his death somehow triggered their own?

And what kind of chutzpah did it take for DeSoto to shoot at them in broad daylight and then stroll right into his attorney's office? If, indeed, it was DeSoto who had shot at them. Of course that appointment put him in Macon just before the shooting. But who else would want Belle dead?

Before DeSoto died, she'd thought things were beginning to add up, but now the sum only created more questions. It was like a trigonometric equation. She had solved for x, only to find a second variable, DeSoto and his death, as part of the answer, because, if she'd learned anything, coincidence wasn't common.

She threw back the covers, sat up, and tried to go back over what she knew and didn't know.

Why was Suzanne murdered? If someone knew Suzanne killed Hovey, however it happened, why wasn't she turned over to the police and brought up on charges?

The photos in that box at Suzanne's house. And the photo of Richard in her bedroom. Were there other photos? Had Suzanne caught Richard on film with someone else? Had she tried to blackmail someone?

No. That didn't make sense either. He was an attorney. He openly associated with the scum of the earth. And what woman would find it objectionable to be linked to Richard Hovey? Unless she was married. And even then, she'd have to be married to some really important, powerful person to worry about divorce in this day and age, especially if Richard Hovey were around to represent her and help her put her life back together.

"Hey." The voice was soft and drowsy from behind her, but she still jumped.

"Belle. You scared me."

Belle put a hand on her shoulder and yawned loudly. "What you doin' up?"

"I couldn't sleep. I can't get DeSoto and Suzanne and Hovey out of my mind."

"Sounds pretty crowded in there."

"It is."

"Want to talk about it?" Belle came around, dropped one of the pillows on the floor, and sat down next to Jennifer. She rubbed her face and gave another huge yawn. "By the way, if I haven't already thanked you, I do appreciate what you did for me today. If you hadn't been there, I don't know if I'd have had the presence of mind to get myself out of there. I'm not accustomed to being used for target practice."

"That's okay. I was kind of panicked myself."

"You hungry?"

"Belle, it's. . . ." She lifted her wrist to catch enough light from the kitchen to read the dial. "It's two-thirty in the morning. Do you always snack in the middle of the night?"

"Yeah. Don't you? Besides, you know Chinese doesn't stick with you. I'll fix us some PB and J."

"And I'll get us some milk. You'll need some help with that sore hand of yours."

"No, I'm fine. You stay put. Your kitchen's so small, one person can barely turn around in it, let alone two. I'll call you when the food's ready."

Belle did have a nicer side. She had to for Sam to have ever spent time with her. And, at last, Jennifer was seeing a little of it.

"Have you slept at all?" Belle called from the kitchen.

"Not really. I just can't let all this go." She went around the partition and watched Belle dip peanut butter and spread it onto the bread. "Chunky."

"I picked some up this past morning while you were out. Oh, I know. I wasn't supposed to leave the apartment, but I just dashed up the road, and chunky's so much better than smooth."

Jennifer watched as Belle glopped on the jelly. "Do you know how decadent that is?"

"Sure. And you don't even want to know how many calories are in it." Belle added the top bread, cut the sandwich diagonally and handed the plate to Jennifer. "Go ahead. Don't wait for me." She pulled two more slices out of the bread bag.

What was still bothering her was how someone could get that kind of dose of sleeping pills into someone like Suzanne without her knowing it.

Jennifer took a bite of sandwich and then put it down. She needed milk. "Do you mind?" she asked Belle. "I need to get past you to get to the refrigerator."

Jennifer backed up and Belle stepped out, knife in hand, and exchanged places while Jennifer grabbed the milk jug out of the fridge and poured them both a glass.

"I'll let you back in," Jennifer offered.

"That's okay. Just pass the jar over here."

Jennifer scooted the peanut butter jar

and her milk over to Belle as Belle passed her her sandwich.

"Too bad we don't have a bottle of wine," Jennifer added, leaning back against the counter. "Two glasses and I'm gone. What kind of wine goes with peanut butter and jelly? Maybe a good white zinfandel?"

"No, red would go better, don't you think?" Belle suggested. "I could use a glass of cabernet sauvignon."

Jennifer took another nibble of sandwich and a bit of peanut butter stuck to her tooth. She fished it loose with her tongue. And as she did, her eyes met Belle's. Solemn, serious, intently watching her.

The truth struck her full in the face. The Silver Oak that was Richard Hovey's favorite wine was a cabernet sauvignon.

How could she have been so dense? Like minds. Both were risky, attractive, intense. Of course Hovey would fall for Belle. And she for him. She wouldn't pester him with morals. She didn't have any.

And she knew why Belle had come to stay in Macon: To watch over Sam. To make sure he didn't figure it all out. To make sure Richard hadn't let something slip about her in the interviews he'd given Sam. Their relationship was to remain secret until they were ready to tell his family and the rest of the world. And now it had to remain secret so her name would never be linked to Hovey's should someone figure out that Suzanne had been murdered.

And she knew that Belle knew that she knew.

"Eat up, Jennifer. You need to get some sleep."

"So do you."

Belle slipped her hand into the pocket of her robe.

Jennifer scanned the counters. Knives in a butcher's block. Dull knives, but knives. Skewers in one of the drawers. A blade in the food processor. The remnants of last night's Chinese dinner. There had to be chopsticks somewhere in that mess of paper. The number of weapons in that kitchen was overwhelming. Exactly what did Belle plan to do? Of course, she could have a little gun tucked in that pocket, the one her hand was in.

"Sam would have let it go eventually," Belle said. "Everybody was just glad to be rid of Suzanne."

Not everybody. Not Suzie. Not Kelli. Not Marjorie.

"But you don't know when to stop, do you?" Belle went on. "You're the worrying type. Something doesn't fit, something doesn't quite make sense, and it will keep after you until you figure it out."

"That's right," Jennifer agreed, raising the sandwich to her lips. She opened her mouth to take another bite. And then she stopped. Peanut butter. Chunky peanut butter. God. It was in the peanut butter. That's how she'd drugged Suzanne. How much had she already had? It couldn't be more than one pill, surely. It hadn't been that big a bite. She dropped the sandwich back onto the plate.

Belle lifted her hand from the pocket of her robe, a gun in her fist, just as Jennifer suspected. Not all that original a backup plan, but then nobody said Belle was a genius.

"I really think you should finish that sandwich."

"Oh, I'm sure you do, so you can take my body elsewhere and try to pass off my death as another unsolved murder. Or accident. Surely not another suicide. That one's getting old."

"Haven't you heard? There's a murderer on the loose. Someone killed Simon DeSoto, the same person who tried to kill me this afternoon."

"I hate to spoil your plan, but if I die,

Belle, it's going to be right here, right in this apartment with plenty of evidence that you were the one who did it."

Chapter 32

"Eat the damn sandwich," Belle growled, blocking the only way out of the little slit of a kitchen.

"Not yet. I want to know why you killed Suzanne."

"She killed Richard."

"Surely it was an accident."

"Surely I don't give a damn how or why she did it. All I know is when I got to his house late Saturday night, he was dead at the bottom of the stairs. When I went upstairs, I saw what she'd done. That bitch had tried to seduce him."

"How'd you know it was her?"

"She'd been calling him off and on for months. Nothing too pushy, but I knew she'd pull something eventually. I deal with nuts like her every day. Their behavior escalates."

"Why didn't Richard take out a restraining order against her?"

"And validate her existence? He was convinced she'd go away, that she was harmless."

"But you weren't."

"I kept watch on her."

"Because you thought he might be cheating on you."

"A man cheats on his wife with a mistress. Why in the world would the mistress think he would be true to her?"

So Hovey had been cheating on Ruth. With Belle.

"She shouldn't. You had a key to his place."

"Of course. You have one to Sam's, don't you?"

She didn't but she nodded anyway.

"And I found him. Dead. His neck badly broken."

"If you'd called 911, he might have been revived."

"No. He was dead. And even if something could have been done, Richard wouldn't have wanted to live that way, not as a cripple. You didn't know him."

"I still don't understand why you didn't call the police."

"And let that bitch get off? I know what lawyers can do. I was about to marry one of the best. She would never have served a day. Accident, insanity, whatever. She would have walked and you know it."

"But why stage Suzanne's elaborate suicide?"

"Two reasons. I waited four days. I actually gave her a chance to come forward, turn herself in, but she didn't. When I knocked on her door Wednesday night, she was a mess."

"How did you go to her house without anybody seeing you?"

"I pulled off the road and hiked over to the house, in the dark. She had all that wedding nonsense strewn all over the living room."

"I can't believe she let you in."

"Why not? I told her I had been in love with Richard, too. She already knew that. I'd told her off one time on the phone when she'd called his house. I gave her some bullshit about knowing how much Richard loved her."

"And she bought it?"

"You kidding? It was what she was telling me. She must have had half a dozen condolence phone calls — for my fiancé — while I was sitting there. She was pathetic, really, but halfway convincing.

"I'd brought a bottle of Southern Comfort. She was more than happy to share it with me, although she did most of the drinking. And then I offered to make her a peanut butter and jelly sandwich. I'd brought my own peanut butter and jelly. Comfort food."

"But why the setup and why on his grave?"

"Like I said, you should have seen that room. I figured if I was going to kill her, why not give her the wedding she always wanted?"

"How'd you get her dressed?"

"She was drunk. She wanted to go to Richard's grave to pay her respects. I got her into the bedroom to help me look for something appropriate for her to wear. I suggested white. After all, she was his bride to be. That summer dress was the only white item she owned. I helped her get into it, and then I found a blue ribbon and combed her hair for her. She showed me the shoes. She'd bought them for her wedding. The pills were kicking in by then, and I was afraid she'd pass out on me before I got her into her car, but I managed."

"What about the suicide note?"

"I brought it with me. Laying her out on his grave was a last-minute inspiration. I'd just planned to do her in at her house."

"What about the white satin shoes and the tape player?"

"After I strapped her into the passenger

seat, I went back into the house for them. And the empty whiskey bottle. I had the pill bottle in my pocket. I found the linen cloth in a closet. I stopped for the roses at an all-night grocery. I was just lucky they had white."

"While Suzanne waited in the car."

"Slept in the car."

"And the song? 'All You Need Is Love'?"

Belle smiled. "Appropriate, don't you think? She had it playing when I got there. Suzanne didn't need a man, only love."

"You drove to the graveyard, moved the flower arrangements out of the way, spread the cloth, and —"

"Went back and got Suzanne out of the car. She was totally out of it by then, but she could still walk with me holding her up. I took off her coat, laid her down, changed her shoes, and put the flowers in her hands. I dropped the pill bottle and hefted the whiskey bottle out a ways."

"Then what did you do?"

"I walked over to the gas station below the cemetery, called a cab, and had it drop me off at the Starvin' Marvin near Suzanne's home. Then I hiked back in the dark to her house, let myself back into her unlocked house, put away her coat and shoes, and picked up my car."

It was horrible to think of Suzanne helping Belle murder her, but Jennifer couldn't dwell on that, not now.

"The little enamel anklet. That was yours."

"Something borrowed. I took it off my own ankle and put it on Suzanne's. I decided she could keep it. And now it's your turn," Belle said. "Eat."

"No."

"I'll shoot you."

"You do that. And then what will you do?"

"I'll make it look as if an intruder broke in."

"The same one who tried to kill you, excuse me, tried to kill me in the parking lot? No wonder you were so angry. You weren't supposed to get hurt. What was the signal? Once you went down between the cars he was supposed to shoot? I was the one out in the open. I should have realized it at the time. And here I was trying to protect you. You must have had a real laugh over that one."

"I was too pissed. The idiot missed."

"And the intruder story . . . That won't work. That lock on my door is a bar lock, remember? It goes all the way across the frame. Once it's thrown, nobody can get in short of hacking down the door."

"You were tired and you forgot to put it on."

"When Sam left, he waited to hear it slide into place."

"Okay then. I woke up and needed some air. I went outside and when I came back, I neglected to put it on. Or the intruder had already slipped inside. It was so foolish of me. I'm so terribly sorry, but it was an accident. I'll never forgive myself."

"Yeah? Well, I appreciate the sentiment. Where were we?"

"You were dead."

"Not dead. Wounded." Jennifer studied the gun. "That's a .22 pistol. You should have brought something bigger. Oh, I know they're more bulky and you were packing light, but you're going to have to hit me more than once."

"Not if it's well placed."

"It won't be. What do you think I'm going to do, just stand here and let you shoot me? We're going to be struggling, and I plan to hurt you, leave some of your blood on me as evidence. So you're going to have to put at least two bullets in me, probably three. And you'll have my blood all over you. How are you going to explain that to the police? They're going to know you did it."

"All right then, I'll wound myself."

"In the arm or the leg? Better make it the arm. You might hit an artery in the leg and then bleed to death. And how are you going to explain away the powder residue on your hand?"

"I was sleeping. I heard noise out here. A scream and then shots. I came out and struggled with our assailant. You, unfortunately, were already dead. In our struggle, we fell against you, struggled over you. I managed to get my hand around the gun, and —"

"And what? Shot yourself?"

"I was shot and he fled."

"Leaving no DNA, no hair, no fibers behind."

"I'm sure there're all sorts of fibers in this apartment for them to choose from. You don't keep the most spotless house, you know."

Terrific. She'd just helped Belle perfect her plan.

"You're pretty good at this," Belle said.

"Yeah, well it's sort of what I do. But you forgot about the gun."

"I'll get rid of it before the police get here."

"I do have neighbors."

"Even better. It'll take them awhile to get out of bed and when they do come see what's going on, I'll make sure they all come in to see your body and leave their fibers."

"Muffy," Jennifer called. She let out a whistle.

"Don't bother," Belle told her, a nasty grin on her face. "She likes peanut butter, too."

Chapter 33

"Nobody messes with Muffy." Jennifer threw herself on top of Belle. They crashed to the floor, hitting the linoleum so hard she heard the air leave Belle's lungs in one loud grunt. Her leg began to bleed again. She felt the wet stickiness seeping into the gauze, but that was the least of her problems.

"You bitch," Belle gasped in Jennifer's ear. "I think I broke something."

"I certainly hope so." She could feel the gun wedged tightly against her chest, where she was going to have one heck of a bruise, assuming she lived to check it out. And she could feel Belle's hand, still firmly wrapped around the grip.

"I can still pull the trigger," Belle warned.

"I don't think that would be good for either one of us."

Suddenly Belle bent her right leg and rolled, throwing Jennifer hard against the lower cabinets. But she was right back on top of her. Where else did she have to go?

She grabbed Belle's wrist and a shot rang past her ear.

Belle's mouth was moving, spitting words, but Jennifer couldn't make out any of them. She twisted and threw herself full force against Belle's right shoulder, and this time, the gun fell from her hand.

Belle managed to grab it with her bandaged left hand, but she couldn't force her gauze-wrapped finger around the trigger. To keep Jennifer from taking it from her, she flung it over her shoulder. It skittered toward the dining table and into the darkness. Jennifer's ringing ear gave her no indication where it went after that.

She managed to push herself up so she was straddling Belle. Belle caught her with an uppercut to the stomach that held as much force as she could manage from a prone position. She slapped Belle hard on the cheek, fully aware that the lock on her door, so carefully designed to keep people out of her apartment, even police, may have sealed Muffy's fate. They could beat up on each other for hours, but unless someone got hold of that gun, lost in the darkness, or she did something clever, Muffy was going to die.

She had one thing going for her: the hometown advantage. She pushed hard against Belle's shoulders and pushed herself upright, rocking back onto her feet, and turned. Belle scrambled up behind her, but not before she managed to open the cabinet door next to the stove. She reached inside, pulled out a box of salt, and flipped it open. Belle grabbed her upper arm, and as Belle pulled her round to face her, she flung a stream of crystals at her face, right into Belle's very surprised eyes.

Belle screamed, a bloodcurdling screech. Jennifer shoved past her as Belle fumbled for the sink. She dashed to the door and flipped on the overhead lights to the dining area and the living room. Now where the heck was that gun? She got down on all fours and wasted precious seconds scrambling around the table legs, but she couldn't find it.

Back to the door to release the bar and push it out of the way, then unlock the dead bolt and finally the small lock on the door handle itself.

"Don't move."

Jennifer turned, her hand still on the doorknob, cradling it behind her back, to see Belle, her eyes swollen and red, holding the pistol in a shaky hand. "I should have killed you in your sleep."

"Probably," Jennifer agreed. "But I think it's a little late for that now." She looked Belle up and down. "Lots of comingled DNA all over you and all over me. You look like hell, by the way. How are you going to explain all this to the police?"

The muffled whir in the distance was growing louder and louder.

"My neighbor, Mrs. Ramon, the one across the hall who you and Sam kept bothering the other day? She's from El Salvador. She knows the difference between a backfire and a gunshot."

Chapter 34

Jennifer stared through the glass window of the surgery room at the Macon Small Animal Clinic and felt the tears stream down her cheeks. Muffy lay so still on the table, an IV hooked to her leg.

Mrs. Ramon patted her shoulder, giving her a little hug every now and again. She held her rosary in her hands.

"Is she going to be all right?" Sam's voice whispered behind her.

She turned and there he stood in the brightly lit, sterile hallway holding a Scooby Doo balloon almost as big as Muffy herself in one hand and a huge bone with a red bow around it and a bag of Snausages in the other.

She couldn't help but grin, and the tears started all over again. Mrs. Ramon cocked her head toward Sam and gave her a little push in his direction.

But it didn't take much. She threw her arms around his waist and hugged him tight, burying her face in his shoulder. "I muff ooo."

"What'd you say?" he asked.

She looked up at him, suddenly self-conscious. "Thank God you're here."

Sam dropped the treats and the bone and let the balloon float to the ceiling. He took her face in his hands. "How is she?"

Jennifer pulled back a little and wiped her tears with the heel of her hand. "They pumped her stomach. They think they got enough of the pills and the peanut butter out. She does have some in her system that she's just going to have to sleep off. That's why they are keeping her overnight, so they can monitor her and make sure she'll be all right."

"That's great, but do you think we can get back to what you said before you started telling me about Muffy. I'm not sure I heard you right."

The lump in her throat was huge. "Sam, we can't talk about this here. I'm exhausted and —"

"You look like hell." He ran his finger over her cheek. "You have bruises —"

"In places you can only imagine."

He grinned.

"Stop that!" She slapped his arm. "I have to get down to the police station. They were gracious enough to let me make sure Muffy would be all right."

Mrs. Ramon snorted. "She made the paramedics look at Muffy before her." The woman threw up her hands. "And then one of the police officers, he rush us here in his squad car."

"You wouldn't let me come by myself."

"Jennifer, I'm so sorry," Sam said. "I would never have let Belle in your place if I'd had any idea. . . ."

"I know you wouldn't. Hey, it's all right. Really. She killed Suzanne and hired someone to shoot me. Surely she didn't kill DeSoto as well."

"The casings that were recovered in the wooded area near your apartment match ones found in the alley where DeSoto's body was found. Police think they're looking for the same shooter."

"But why DeSoto?"

"All I can figure is that Belle's story had begun to fall apart, and she couldn't afford to have the police question him, especially after she'd had you shot at. She'd passed off the break-in at her apartment, the one at mine, and then the shooting as DeSoto's doings although I don't think she mentioned his name when the police questioned her. If she had, they would have picked him up. He was bound to defend himself, and a polygraph test would show he was telling the truth."

"So DeSoto never was a danger?"

"Nope. His attorneys released a statement following his death saying they intended to go forward to clear his name of the charges pertaining to the murder of his wife. Their theory is that the alleged hit man wasn't a hit man at all, but DeSoto's wife's jealous lover. The phone calls to their residence were made to her, not him. The lovers had a falling-out, and he killed her. The police were suspicious of DeSoto because they always have to check out the spouse in a case of murder like that, especially where there's insurance involved, and there was a lot of insurance. They found the lover/hit man fairly easily through the phone records —"

"Then Belle didn't have anything to do with that."

"No. When he was arrested, the lover insisted that DeSoto had set the whole thing up, that he'd never met Mrs. DeSoto. He had some weapons and drug charges in the past, so they lent his story some credibility. That gave him a twenty-year plea bargain and left DeSoto taking the lion's share of responsibility for the murder."

"But then why did Belle have letters

postmarked from prison?"

"My guess is that part of her story was true, that she really was trying to get DeSoto's confession in writing."

"But wouldn't that be a betrayal of Hovey? He was the man's attorney."

"Only if she used it."

"Right. Hovey marries her and she wins big time. He dumps her and she's got one heck of a news story and a terrific way to screw him over, by proving his client guilty with his own words."

"Excuse me." Mrs. Ramon tapped Jennifer's shoulder. "Enough store chat."

"Shop talk," Sam corrected.

"You do better to tend to your business than teach me your phrases. Look." She pointed through the glass at Muffy. "You see?"

One of her ears twitched. Then she lifted her head and let out a low, pitiful whine.

Jennifer had the door open and was at her side in less than ten seconds. "There, there, baby, it's okay." She rubbed the dog's neck, and Muffy's tail thumped against the table. Jennifer checked to make sure the IV was still securely in place. It was well taped, not likely to come loose.

Sam was right behind her, tying the balloon to the end of the cart. Muffy gave a sniff in its direction and let out a soft growl.

"What's the matter, girl. You don't like Scooby? Come on. He's one of your own, part of the Mystery Machine." He popped open the bag of Snausages and snuck her one. That got her tail wagging again.

"Quit that," Jennifer warned. "You shouldn't be feeding her without the doctor's permission. And you're just about to get busted." She pointed to a woman in a white coat, being led down the hall by Mrs. Ramon.

The vet came through the door and went straight to Muffy. "So how are you feeling?" She turned to Jennifer. "Give me about two seconds to look her over and then she's all yours."

"You mean I can take her home?"

"Of course. Just look at her. We'd have to sedate her to keep her here. Muffy's going to be just fine."

Chapter 35

Jennifer continued to grumble at Teri all the way from the car to Monique's front door. "I can't imagine what could be so important that you have to drag me over here when you know that I need to watch over Muffy —"

"Mrs. Ramon will treat her like her own child," Teri assured her.

"I know that, but Muffy only got a few hours' sleep last night, or should I say this morning, after we finally got her home. And then when we tried to nap this afternoon, you woke us up with your phone call. What's happened? I don't think I can take one more crisis."

Monique had the door open before they had the chance to ring the bell. She shushed Jennifer, who, as usual, had her mouth open, and shuffled them through the house and into the kitchen.

"Surprise!" a chorus shouted.

The room was full of balloons, all loose and floating against the ceiling with long, colorful, curled ribbons hanging from them almost to the floor, making it difficult to see exactly who was in the room.

"What's this?" Jennifer gasped.

"It's an It's-Good-to-Be-Alive party!" Leigh Ann tackle-hugged her from behind. "Dee Dee sent over a cake. Isn't it beautiful? She's so sorry she couldn't come but she had that party tonight she had to cater."

"Oh, no. I was supposed to help her with that. I completely forgot."

"It's okay," Teri assured her. "She understands that near-death experiences require a little downtime."

This was downtime?

"Margaritas for everyone!" April declared. She was over next to the stove, sticky-looking goo all over her hands, using a spatula to scoop a frothy pink icy mixture out of the blender and into seven crystal Margarita glasses sitting on Monique's kitchen counter.

"Those are not Margaritas," Teri insisted. "Margaritas are not strawberry sugar drinks. I don't see any salt. Did you put any tequila in them?"

"Okay then, Miss Party-pooper Teri. Strawberry daiquiris! Come and get 'em."

"April, they don't have any rum in them

either," Monique reminded her, picking up one of the glasses.

April raised her drink in Jennifer's direction, not about to let anyone, not even Monique, dampen this celebration. "To our Jennifer and Muffy's savior."

Leigh Ann raised her glass and chanted, "Go, Jen. Go, Jen. Go, Jen."

"Enough already." But Jennifer couldn't help but smile. They were all crazy, but in a good way.

Jennifer heard a small, ladylike cough come from a chair in the corner of the room. Half covered by balloons sat Mrs. Walker, looking tiny and fragile.

Most deceptive.

"I know," Jennifer said to her. "You told me so."

"Oh, heavens, dear, I never utter that phrase. I've had it said to me so many times I've thought of having it copyrighted so that no one could use it without my permission. I'm just delighted you saw that Belle woman for what she was before you made a meal of that peanut butter and jelly sandwich. Snacking in the middle of the night . . ." She shook her head and made a *tsk*ing sound with her tongue. "Most unhealthy. I say we drink these delightful confections that April has so graciously put together for us," Leigh Ann handed her a drink, "and then you let me make the next round. I make a killer Manhattan."

"I second that," Teri muttered.

"To Jennifer." Monique raised her glass and they each took a sip.

A sip was all Jennifer could manage. It was like drinking snow-cone syrup.

"Now I know this is supposed to be a celebration," Mrs. Walker said, "but I simply must know. Was Belle actually after Sam, romantically, I mean?"

"Yeah, I want to know that, too." Leigh Ann came up behind and threw a big handful of confetti over Jennifer's head.

"I don't think so, but she wouldn't have been above pretending to be."

"Sam is way too honest for the likes of Belle," April, busy washing the blender at the sink, called over her shoulder.

"I bet she was none too pleased when she found she'd have to deal with you," Monique sniffed.

"I'm sure she wasn't," Jennifer agreed. "Belle and Sam had given a relationship a try, and they both knew it wasn't right. But she and Hovey seemed a good match. I think she was as in love with him as she could have been with anybody. They'd been super careful not to let their relationship leak out for fear of the ruckus Ruth would raise. They were going to slip away and get married and then announce it to the world, but —"

"Hovey's dying put a little kink in that plan," Teri interrupted.

"Right," Jennifer went on, "and with Suzanne dead, she was desperate to know what Hovey had said to Sam in those interviews, whether or not he'd mentioned her — Belle — directly or indirectly, because if he had, someone might question her in respect to Suzanne's death. The engagement announcement was something she knew Sam wouldn't ignore, couldn't ignore, however he felt about her."

"She had to resent him, too," Monique added.

"Why?" Jennifer asked.

"Hovey asked him to coauthor his memoirs, and Belle was a perfectly competent journalist."

With a smeared reputation. That would hurt.

"So who broke into Sam's apartment?" Leigh Ann asked.

"Nobody," Jennifer explained. "Belle messed up her own stuff and his door, and then stole Sam's computer files and tapes.

She didn't count on him having an unlabeled backup disk. Or even that he'd notice they were gone, at least not right away. But if he did, the break-in would cover it, and she could blame it on DeSoto, like she did everything else. Not that Sam would have caught the reference to the trips she and Hovey had made. It's funny how something nobody would notice can seem so glaring when you know its significance."

"But you noticed it. So that's why she tried to kill you," Teri said, pouring her Margarita down the sink.

"Actually I think it was because she knew I was convinced Suzanne had been murdered. If I'd left it alone, she would have checked Sam's files and been out of here, convinced she was home free."

"So who actually shot at you?" April asked, pausing to take another sip of her drink. At least half of her strawberry confection was already gone.

"Anyone checked out my buddy Burt?" Teri asked.

"The police went looking for him after I gave them his name. According to Ruth, he worked for Hovey before he was killed, so we know Belle knew him. Ruth sort of inherited him, but she made it clear his position with her was only temporary. Guess that's why he was looking for jobs on the side. And, guess what? He's mysteriously disappeared."

"Fancy that." Teri batted a balloon that had floated right in front of her face.

"But why frame DeSoto, dear?" Mrs. Walker asked. "He seemed awfully convenient."

"If she hadn't used DeSoto, she would have used one of the other clients Hovey had recently gotten out on bail, or perhaps some other inmate who had just been released. Sam found out that she corresponded with most of them, looking for that elusive story that was going to make her career."

"I bet Hovey loved her writing inmates," Leigh Ann added.

"I'm sure he didn't know about it. The police found all kinds of letters when they searched her apartment."

"Oh, goodness. She was a rather reckless young woman," Mrs. Walker observed.

"Quite."

"And the death threat you told us she had received . . ." Mrs. Walker began.

"That was something Belle put together herself. I'm sure she never intended to actually get DeSoto involved, but events began to snowball. He was a convenient fall guy."

"Did Suzanne put that item in the newspaper announcing her wedding to Hovey herself?" Teri asked.

"According to the newspaper office she did. My guess is she had decided, once and for all, to seduce him, after which she was convinced Hovey would admit his undying love for her. The announcement was scheduled to come out several days later, after it would all be official. Remember, this was Suzanne's fantasy she was living out."

"Dear me, I don't suppose we'll ever know exactly what happened that night," Mrs. Walker said.

Jennifer shook her head. "The only two people who know are both dead, but I'd like to think it was an accident, that Suzanne wouldn't have intentionally killed Richard."

"Oh, oh, oh. You're forgetting the engagement ring that Hovey bought," Leigh Ann insisted.

"The ring was obviously for Belle," Teri said.

"Well, yeah. But why didn't she wear it?" April asked from the sink.

"Have you not heard anything that

Jennifer's been telling us?" Teri asked. "She couldn't. No one was supposed to know they were engaged."

"I was running water. Cleaning up after all of you," April said.

"None of you saw that ring," Leigh Ann broke in. "No way I could put that in some drawer and not wear it."

The doorbell rang, and Monique excused herself. She immediately came back with Suzie Turner in tow, looking more than a little overwhelmed by all the balloons. She went directly to Jennifer and threw her arms around her.

"I can't stay but a minute. I got someone to cover for me. I couldn't miss your party. Mrs. Dupree said you'd want to see me."

Jennifer closed her eyes and hugged Suzie to her. She felt the tears start down her cheeks. "Suzie, I'm sorry. I wish things had been different. I wish —"

"It's okay. Really." Suzie pulled back. "Aunt Suzanne didn't mean to kill Mr. Hovey."

"I'm sure she didn't," Jennifer agreed.

"That's why she was afraid to die, wasn't it?" Suzie asked.

"I think so."

"She prayed about it, I know she did.

Made her peace with God. Before she died." She managed a small smile. "I told you she wouldn't have left me without saying good-bye."

Chapter 36

"Hmmmmmm," Sam said, holding Jennifer close on the dance floor of the Casablanca Club. Santana's "Love of My Life" was playing in the background.

He looked wonderful in a charcoal gray suit, but just as mischievous as ever and not about to help her out.

She'd opted for a black dress in a Chinese cut. It covered most of her bruises.

"I liked the flowers," he said.

"Did you?"

"A dozen red roses. Nice. I must admit I was surprised when you called yesterday evening and made the date," Sam whispered in her ear. "I didn't think you'd be up to it. What did you mean when you said 'We need to talk'?"

She supposed she deserved that. Heck, she deserved a lot more. If she'd let him talk last Saturday night like he'd wanted to, who knows how it would have changed the events of the past week. And that night.

"Sam, I'm not any good at this and you

know it. I don't know how to act. I don't know what to say. I'm surprised I'm actually allowed out on dates."

"Hyperbole."

"Yeah, well, it's how I'm feeling right now. Scared. You have to understand that I'm comfortable with my life. I know what to do each morning when I wake up. I write. I take care of Muffy and myself. I help Dee Dee with her catering. I check the mail. I hope something I've sent out will finally be bought and I —"

"And what if it does get bought, Jennifer? Your life could change with one letter or one phone call. Then what would you do?"

She'd never actually thought about it. "I don't know. I've done this so long, ever since I graduated from college. I can't imagine anything different."

"And what do you want for us?" he asked.

"I don't know that either. I'm not good at looking ahead." All she really knew was what she didn't want. She didn't want to lose Sam, couldn't bear to even think of her life without him.

"We can ease into this, Jennifer," Sam suggested. "Just say it. The first time's the hardest, but once you get the hang of it, it just rolls off your tongue. I know because I've said it probably a thousand times by now, just not where you could hear me. C'mon, I'll show you."

He stopped swaying and cupped her chin with his hand and looked at her with those deep, dark blue eyes of his. "I love you, Jennifer Adele Marsh. I've been trying to tell you that for what seems like a long, long time. Whew! There. See? Not really all that hard. I feel like a kid who's just lifted his feet for the first time on his two-wheeler and is soaring down the road with no idea how to stop the thing. I think I can even say it louder. Shout it to everyone in the room."

Sam drew in a great breath, but Jennifer covered his mouth with her fingers.

"I . . . I love you, Sam."

There. Now she'd said it. Out loud. And nothing horrible had happened. No thunder crashes, no earthquakes.

"I really do," she said, "but. . . ."

"But what? Why does there have to be a *but?* No conditions, Jennifer. It's a simple idea. We'll take it slow, if that's what we need to do, but I don't want any more guessing. I want to know that you feel as strongly about me as I feel about you."

She swallowed hard. "I do, Sam, I do.

It's just that I can't plan anything yet. I'm just not ready —"

"We've got our plans. We're writing Hovey, Belle, and Suzanne's story. You and me together, including a firsthand account of how you personally foiled your own murder and unmasked Belle as Suzanne's killer."

"And Belle will no doubt be writing her own account. From prison — if she sees a day in jail."

"If she's convicted, she won't be allowed to profit from her crime, which means Marjorie and Suzie should get the proceeds from anything she produces. Either way, if she does write it, we'll have even more publicity for our book."

"I haven't been able to get my mysteries published, Sam. I'm sure you think —"

"That you're brilliant." He twirled her and she let out a little squeal. He drew her back to him. "Sorry. Forgot for a moment there that you'd been fighting off the bad guys. Fiction takes time. I know. I'm still trying to peddle my short stories."

"You? You never shared that with me. I want to read them."

He shrugged. "They're only stories. You write novels."

Sam felt self-conscious about showing

her his work? Life truly was strange.

"I think it's time we put together a strategy plan to get you published. I've got several ideas that might help. As a matter of fact I think we should present our non-fiction proposal along with your Maxie Malone books as a package deal."

"You'd do that for me?"

"Of course. For us. Any publisher would be an idiot to pass them up. 'Mystery writer exposes web of intrigue surrounding death of nationally known attorney Richard Hovey.' Something along those lines. Jennifer, we're a team."

Oh, how she did love that man.

"So what about us? What were you going to say to me last Saturday night? It was so lovely. I'm so sorry I spoiled the evening."

"I'm not pushing for more of a commitment than the one you've just given me."

She'd almost been hoping he was. Not that it wouldn't make her panic.

"I don't know why I'm so gun-shy, Sam."

"You're just scared. Hell, I'm scared, too. You're scared because when you say something you mean it. And when you make a promise, it's for all time, not just for tomorrow or next week or until things get rough."

"I do. I do love you. I just don't know what will happen."

"And neither do I. That's the fun of it." He grinned. "All you have to be concerned about is tonight and tomorrow and the day after."

She hugged him tight. She could handle that. Tonight, tomorrow, and the day after that.

We hope you have enjoyed this Large Print book. Other Thorndike, Wheeler or Chivers Press Large Print books are available at your library or directly from the publishers.

For more information about current and upcoming titles, please call or write, without obligation, to:

Publisher
Thorndike Press
295 Kennedy Memorial Drive
Waterville, ME 04901
Tel. (800) 223-1244

Or visit our Web site at:
www.gale.com/thorndike
www.gale.com/wheeler

OR

Chivers Press, Limited
Windsor Bridge Road
Bath BA2 3AX
England
Tel. (01225) 335336

Or visit Chivers Web site at
www.chivers.co.uk

All our Large Print titles are designed for easy reading, and all our books are made to last.